RIGHT-HAND MAN

CONNIE WILLIAMS

Publisher's Note

Many children today face the problem of losing a parent and having to accept a new person in that role. It is a stressful situation that fills the child with turmoil, even though he may seem to be handling everything well.

In *Right-Hand Man,* Sam prays for Mom-Jo to get a husband, but he reacts negatively to the prospect of actually acquiring a stepfather. It takes time for him to sort out his feelings and deal with his private doubts, and he cannot help worrying that his close relationship with Mom-Jo will be threatened.

Eventually, he comes to understand her viewpoint as well as his own needs, and the transition is accomplished through his future stepfather's gentleness and patience.

Sam uses a vigorous, take-the-bull-by-the-horns approach in trying to solve his problems; his comments are by turns sobering and hilarious; and his story will provide the reader with insight as well as enjoyment.

Contents

Chapter One
Two Mr. Rights

The football was flying straight toward the back of Mom-Jo's head. "Watch out!" I yelled.

It skipped across the top of her head and bounced crookedly in the grass. She whirled around. "Blake and Georgie!" she said.

They were hiding behind the Clancy family, who sat like four stones on their lawn chairs.

"Blake and Georgie," she repeated sternly as she marched toward my two little brothers.

I decided to go after the football. It had stopped beside Mr. and Mrs. Davis, who were holding hands while they watched the soccer game. Their two little kids were sitting on a blanket, playing with coloring books and cars.

I picked up the football and turned around. Mom was making Blake and Georgie sit on the ground beside her chair. "Just once I would like to watch your sister play soccer without getting beaned or something,'' she said. ''You sit here by my chair until the game is over.''

I tossed the football into the chair.

''Oh, Sam,'' Mom said to me. ''Please retire the football. Put it in the car trunk.'' She threw me the keys. I scooped up the football and headed toward the car.

On the way back I noticed that Blake and Georgie were wrestling in the grass. The Davis children continued to sit quietly on their blanket. I wondered if they behaved like that because they had a dad to help keep them in line. Mrs. Davis stood close to her husband. She had such a smile of contentment on her face. Mom-Jo looked like she was ready to whack somebody.

That's when I decided that Mom-Jo needed a husband. She needed someone to help her whip Blake and Georgie into shape. She needed someone to hold her hand and make her smile during soccer games.

Then I remembered my teacher, Mrs. Christie, telling us how to get a job done. ''Don't just stand around and think about it,'' she'd said. ''Get up and move. Just take the bull by the horns and do it!''

''Sometimes you just have to take the bull by the horns,'' I said aloud. I needed to catch a husband for Mom-Jo.

I already knew what kind of man Mom needed because I knew her inside out and backwards and upside-down, having lived under her roof for over four of my twelve years. She needed someone rich because she deserved nice things, and she needed someone handsome because she was pretty. And she needed someone who liked kids—because Mom-Jo had four of us.

I spotted the future husband right away. The man climbed out of a light blue Mercedes, and he was tanned like he'd been to Hawaii, or someplace expensive. Being a man myself, I couldn't judge if a girl would think he was handsome, but to me he looked mighty fine, with broad shoulders and a thick neck. And his clothes looked like they matched on purpose. Surely, Mom would think he was handsome. Besides all that, I already knew the husband prospect was available because he was Mary Shore's dad, and he was single.

I watched Mr. Shore while he walked to the second soccer field, where Mary was playing. I left Karin's game and followed the man until he stopped. I went right up to him, sort of like taking the bull by the horns. "Mr. Shore?" I asked.

He looked down at me.

"I'm Samuel Rogers, a friend of Mary's." I stuck out my hand for him to shake.

"Nice to meet you." He shook my hand.

I pointed to Mom, who was looking perplexed at Karin's outstretched form in the grass. Apparently, the ball had slithered into the goal like a greased snake in spite of Karin's quick dive. "Do you see that lady in the pink blouse?" I asked Mr. Shore.

"Yes, I do." He didn't look at me like I was crazy, so I guessed I was doing okay so far.

"Don't you think she's pretty?"

Mom looked relieved now that Karin was standing up and in control again. And Mom also looked real pretty, with her soft blond hair blowing in the breeze. I was glad she'd worn pink today.

"Yes, she's pretty."

"Good."

We just stood there for a few minutes, so I decided to start talking again. "Do you want to meet her?"

He grinned. "Sure."

It took only a few minutes to reach Mom, but by the time we got there I was feeling nervous. "Mom," I said.

She turned to me and smiled.

"This is Mr. Shore."

She looked at him. "Nice to meet you," she said.

"Well, I'll be going." I stuck my hands in my pockets and walked on down to the end of the field where I could watch both the game and Mom with her future husband.

Mom and Mr. Shore seemed to think something was amusing. They chatted and smiled at each other back and forth for a few minutes. I could tell they were getting along real fine. I felt so proud of my matchmaking skills that I began to whistle quietly. Mr. Shore even seemed to lean toward Mom when she talked.

Then Mom looked at him real serious and said something right at his face. I saw his back stiffen, and he took a step away from her. His head continued to nod politely while they talked, but I could tell there was something wrong by the way he left such a clean space between them. Soon he turned and went back to Mary's game, and Mom stood there with her arms hanging down.

I knew then, by her droopy stance, that she would never marry Mr. Shore, and that the reason had to do with the serious statement she had planted on him while he stood beside her. What had she said? Why did it have such an impact? I would ask her later.

Karin's team went to McDonald's after the game, so we went with 'em: me, Mom, Blake, and Georgie. We ordered hamburgers and fries and water. We always order water to drink because there are so many of us, and Mom says it saves us a few bucks if we wait and have our drinks at home later—which usually ends up being milk. When I grow up, my kids'll get soda any time they want.

I couldn't ask Mom about her conversation with Mr. Shore because there were too many people in McDonald's, and so many of 'em were talking to Mom.

Later, I helped her carry the detergent boxes to the basement, but I couldn't ask her about Mr. Shore then because Georgie was crying.

It seems that Blake had told Georgie he was a baby. Since Blake was born a few months before Georgie, Blake always felt like he was real grown up—and Georgie was just a baby. Georgie cried about this every day, and Blake seemed to dig at him harder all the time. "Blake keeps saying, 'Goo-goo,' at me!" Georgie said between sobs.

"Okay," Mom said. "We all need to go upstairs to the living room and hear our story." Mom called it "our story" because it was about us. We'd heard it a million trillion times, but we sat down to hear it again because Mom said it was so important and it would put everything into perspective.

We got settled on the bench across from the piano where the framed pictures were. We had a baby grand that nobody played. It was all loaded up with family pictures, so I guess it was useful for something besides being a clubhouse when you draped blankets over the top.

Mom picked up the photo of my folks. "This is your mom and dad," she said to Karin, Georgie, and me as we all stared at our blond, husky dad and our sweet-smiling mom. Mom-Jo looked at the picture herself. "My oldest sister Margaret, and her husband Phil Rogers."

She set the picture down and chose another one from the collection. "Blake, these are your folks: my second oldest sister Charlotte and Blake Tooley, Sr." We stared at Blake's tall, dark-haired dad with the thick glasses, and his mom with her deep-set, yet friendly, eyes. Mom set this picture down beside the other one.

There used to be another picture there, one of her old fiancé, Doug. Last week when I asked her about him she seemed kind of growly, so I clammed up. But I wondered why his picture wasn't on the piano anymore.

"You are my nephews and niece," she was saying. "I love you like you were my own kids. I'm trying to raise you in a way that would please your folks." Even though the plane crash was almost five years ago, Mom-Jo's eyes always misted up every time she told us "our story," usually at this point. "I miss my sisters."

She looked at all of us. I already knew what she was going to say next. "When we were little, we used to scrap all the time like you do. Please, don't take for granted the precious time spent together." She stared at us real hard, sort of like she wished her eyes could push these important words down into our hearts where they would stick like spears.

Georgie raised his hand. "*Georgie* sounds too little," he said with all his six-year-old intensity. "I can't stand it anymore. I've decided to become someone else."

"What?" I said.

Georgie ignored me. "I want a grown-up name: George Washington."

Mom sighed.

Georgie continued. "Then, when you say, 'George Washington, brush your teeth,' everyone will think you're talking to the president and not to a baby."

"Hey, I like that!" Blake said.

"So, I'm George Washington now," Georgie stated firmly. "I have the same name as the president of the United States."

"He *was* the president, stupid. Now he's dead," Karin commented.

"Shut up," Georgie retorted.

"Do not say 'shut up,' Georgie," Mom said.

"Do not say 'shut up,' *George Washington!*" he shouted.

"Do not use that tone of voice to your mom, George Washington!"

"Of course," he whispered.

Mom turned to Karin. "And don't call your brother 'stupid.' "

"I won't."

I guess Mom realized her speech about getting along so we would appreciate each other was not taking hold. She told everybody to go to bed—all but me.

The other kids scooted on out, and I stayed. Since I was the oldest, Mom often kept me up a bit longer so we could compare notes—as she called it. I was her right-hand man, and the closest thing she had to another adult in the house.

"Samuel," Mom said. "What has been bothering you all evening? You've hardly talked at all, and you've been wiggling your hands in your pockets."

I hadn't thought about it, but she was right. Even as she spoke, my hands were acting like spiders along the seams in my pockets. I thought she had kept me here to laugh with her about Georgie's new name. I held my fingers tight.

"Are you worried about something, Sam?"

Mr. Shore popped right into my head, and my fingers did a little twitch, but I stopped 'em flat. I didn't want Mom to read my mind.

"Did something happen at the soccer game? Or at McDonald's? Speak up."

I decided that maybe I should take the bull by the horns here, and just say what was on my mind. "Mr. Shore said you were pretty." That's all I said.

Mom grinned. "Whose idea was it for him to come talk to me?"

"Both of us, me and Mr. Shore."

She gave me her old "I know" look that made my fingers want to twitch again.

I decided to ask the question that had been bothering me. "What did you say to him that made him go away?"

Her face clouded for a tenth of a second, and then it flitted back to its natural, breezy style. But her eyes looked a little tight. "Don't ask me that question again, son. You wouldn't understand."

Saying "you wouldn't understand" was like dangling a juicy hamburger in front of our dog, Bongo. I *had* to know. "Just tell me," I said.

"No."

"Can I ask you again later? Maybe I'll understand later." Maybe tomorrow.

"No."

"How about when I'm nineteen? Will I understand it then?" I sure didn't like her keeping secrets from me.

Mom smiled her sad smile. "Possibly. Now go to bed, Sam. Don't forget to say your prayers." She patted my shoulder. "I love you." I had been demoted from right-hand man to kid.

When I was in bed, I began to wonder some other things about Mom. I wondered how she had felt when the news came of the plane crash that killed my parents and Blake's on their way to Palm Springs. I remember we were staying with Mom-Jo, who was just our aunt at the time. I remember how sad I felt, and how Blake and Georgie hadn't understood any of it yet. In fact, as time went on, it seemed that the little guys, who were just babies when it happened, adapted real easy to having Mom-Jo be their mom. Karin and I, who were five and seven, went through some lonely times missing our real mom and dad. Now I was used to it—usually.

Tonight, when Mom's eyes misted up, I began to realize how bad she must've hurt when her two sisters died. I'd never thought about it at the time, but now it pinched me real hard inside. How had Mom-Jo managed? Who comforted *her* on the hard nights when she cried—like she'd comforted me?

I didn't want to think about it much, so I turned over onto my other side. Maybe another part of my brain, the one that was uphill now, maybe it would think of something more pleasant to dwell on before I went to sleep. I sighed. Growing up and getting smarter was not always a cheerful procedure. Here I was, unhappy because Mom-Jo had gone through a horrible experience right under my nose, and I'd been too young and stupid to help her. Now it was too late.

Back in the old days when we first became Mom's kids and she was engaged to Doug, he was always around. He was tall and blond, and we liked him. He wrestled with us. I'm sure he helped her some. But he faded away. I'd never thought about it before, but now I wondered if Mom ever missed him. I wondered where he went.

I turned over on my back. Mom had a good life with us kids. We liked her a lot, and our house was big. It was even paid for because it was my folks' house, and they had good financial planning, or something that Mom tried to explain to me once. And we all had trust funds, whatever those are, that paid for stuff like braces and summer camp. She had her job, designing logos for Western Tees and Hats. She had her light table upstairs in the long bedroom. She had her friend Lulu. What did her life lack?

It lacked sisters. And it lacked a husband to help her with the kids. Soon she would be thirty-three. I needed to find her a husband. And I needed to make her not chase him away with the secret words she had used on Mr. Shore.

Lulu came to my rescue. Lulu is Mom's boss. She wears bright red lipstick that comes off on her teeth, and she draws black lines around her eyes. When us kids were little, Lulu used to bring Mom's assignments to the house and pick up the finished work. That way Mom didn't have to pull us out of the sandbox to go to the shop. Sometimes when Lulu came, she passed out candy to everyone and made us eat it outside. Then she would sit down and talk to Mom in the kitchen. They laughed a lot. We all liked Lulu from the start.

The day after Mom's birthday, Karin and I were in the kitchen designing a ramp for marbles. We chose the kitchen because it smelled like warm chocolate chip cookies. Lulu came in and plopped down in her usual spot near the counter.

"Joanna," she said to Mom. "You need a man around." Lulu never beat around the bush; she just whacked it flat from the start.

"I have three men," Mom said, winking at me.

"No, dear. The grown-up kind," Lulu said.

"The kids see Grandpa T. from time to time," Mom said as she shoveled cookies from the pan to the counter. "And they have soccer coaches and Awana and Mr. Murphy next door. And you know how Mike Banner's dad always invites Sam to those father-son things. . . ."

I cringed at the thought of Mike's dad. He always took me along because he felt sorry for me. That's what Mike told me once. And the way he said it made me want to slug him. But you don't just slug your best friend, so I went home and shot baskets instead.

"She's right, Mom," I said. "It's time for you to get a man. I agree with Lulu."

Lulu and Mom looked at each other for a moment before Lulu continued. "I'm inviting you to come have supper with Fred and me next Friday. There's someone we'd like you to meet. He's a friend of ours, in town on business. Seems like he's just your type. You know what I mean—a Christian."

Mom shook her head.

"Go ahead, Mom," I said. "Maybe he's rich and handsome too. I'll baby-sit. I'm twelve now, and I'll only be a phone call away."

Mom looked at me and then at Lulu. "Okay," she said quietly.

On Friday I made sure Mom looked good before she left the house. She had on the navy blue turtleneck sweater that made her eyes look dark, and she had a new skirt from the mall.

She kissed me, gave me Lulu's phone number, told me—for the millionth time—to lock up the house real tight, and left. Even though Lulu and Fred lived only eight blocks away, I was a bit scared when Mom got into the car and drove off, but I didn't let on. A man's got to do what a man's got to do.

First we took the pictures off the piano, lifted the lid, and had a good loud session of piano races. Karin always wins. She can run her fingers up all eighty-eight keys in twenty-five seconds flat.

The kids behaved okay because I told 'em they could have popcorn in the living room. I shouldn't have let them go near the piano, though, especially when its flap was up, because George Washington threw his popcorn into the air to make snow. After they went to bed, I spent an hour digging through piano strings with a walnut picker, and then I put the top down, which I should've done before I served the popcorn. The lid slipped off my hand and banged down with such a loud crash that it woke up Blake and he fell out of bed.

After I got Blake settled again, with my old marble bag on his pillow and his teddy bear tucked under his chin, I set the family pictures back on the piano and stared at the faces that had belonged to my parents. I looked like my mom, I decided, because we both had thin faces and blue eyes, and Karin looked like Dad: blond and serious. I could remember my folks better than the other kids because I was the oldest. Blake and George Washington had no memory of them at all.

My own memory had become somewhat dimmed by time, but not altogether, and I tried to hang on to what I had left: my mother, who smelled and felt and sounded so much like Mom-Jo, and my dad, with his loud voice and wild curls—like Karin's. Mom-Jo said we reminded her of her lost loved ones so much it sometimes made her cry. And other times it made her feel all warm inside because it was like little pieces of them were still here—in us.

I sighed. My mother and dad, and my aunt and uncle. But they were in heaven now with Jesus. It always made me feel better when I reminded myself of that. I looked at the front door and wondered how Mom-Jo was doing at Lulu's supper party.

I heard the car drive up and stop. I heard Mom's footsteps out back, and trash cans being dragged down the driveway. The key scratched in the lock.

"Hi, Sam," Mom said as she entered.

I wouldn't call it a grand entrance. She still looked as pretty as a picture, but tired. She sank down into the couch. "Did Blake go to sleep with his cars on his pillow again? He wakes up with those little tire prints on his cheeks."

"That's all you have to say after a night of romance?" I asked. "Don't let Blake sleep with his face on his cars? He's been doing it for years, Mom." Besides, tonight he was sleeping on the precious marbles.

She sighed, kicked off her shoes, and leaned her head against the back of the couch. "Remember the time he woke up with a crayon sticking out of his ear?" She grinned.

"Mom, how was your evening?" I wanted to know if she was going to get married.

"Very nice. Lulu's friend, Brett, is handsome, athletic, and intelligent. He teaches the adult Sunday school class in his home church."

"Are you going to marry him?"

"Are you my father?"

I smiled. "No, I'm your kid."

"I probably won't see him again."

I couldn't figure it out. She's pretty and she's kind. Why wouldn't the guy see her again? "What did you do? Tell him that stuff I can't hear until I'm nineteen?"

She didn't answer, so I knew she had.

"Why do you say it then, when it chases men away?"

"I'll tell you when you're nineteen."

I bit back a bunch of angry words. "I'll go check Blake's face," I growled.

"Thank you, dear."

I tried to cool off while I marched upstairs to Blake and George Washington's room. It was directly across the hall from Mom's room. I looked in her room first. My real mom and dad had used that room once. Now it belonged to their sister and her artwork center. I opened Blake's door and walked in. As usual, Blake had gathered a whole collection of toys around himself. If he wasn't going to be face-jammed by the little motorcycle near his eyes, his stomach would be wounded by toy guns and blocks. I knocked most of the toys off the bed and shoved them underneath, but I left the bag of marbles on his pillow.

Karin and I slept downstairs, so I went down and peeked into the living room. Mom had her sisters' pictures on her lap. I thought she looked especially sad tonight, and it made my fingers twitch.

I wondered what she had said to Lulu's friend.

I lay in my bed trying to sort it out. I wanted to help Mom so bad. I wanted to find her a rich, handsome man. And I wanted her not to be lonely, and I wanted to know what to do. I sighed. Tonight when I prayed, I would put special emphasis on Mom-Jo and the husband she needed. Come to think of it, maybe God already had one picked out for her. God would know that she deserved someone rich and handsome and kind. . . . I relaxed a bit while I closed my eyes and gave the Mom-Jo–husband situation to the One who knows how to take care of all things.

Chapter Two
Mr. Wrong

The next time Lulu had a man lined up, Mom turned her down. "I can't go to your lunch party, Lulu. Karin has a playoff game on Saturday. Blake and George Washington will be at a birthday party, and I'm looking forward to concentrating on Karin's game without having to constantly pull those two wiggle worms out of trouble."

So, instead of going out with a man to a luncheon on Saturday, Mom put on her favorite royal blue sweater that matched Karin's team and went with me and Karin to the big game.

I'd better explain how Mom watches soccer games. She takes a folding lawn chair, and she sets it near the sidelines somewhere. Then she stands up. When Karin kicks the ball—Mom moves her foot, and when Karin jumps up—Mom does too. I usually like to go with her to the games because not only is she fun to watch, but my buddy Mike Banner has a sister on Karin's team.

Mike was there now, sitting a few yards down the field from Mom's chair. Sometimes Mike and I chased each other around the field or played kickback or threw a football. Today, Mike was watching the game. He'd coughed all night, and his mom wanted him to sit still. I flopped down beside him in the grass.

I looked at Mom. By coming to this game, she was missing ''Mr. Right.'' I wondered if she was upset because of it.

Behind her in the parking lot, a tall man was helping his soccer girl out of a junky-looking gray van. The kid had on a uniform like Karin's, and she ran over to the team. ''That must be the new player,'' I said to Mike.

''Yeah. Her name is Jill. She scored two goals last week.''

While the coach got the girls set up on the field, I noticed the tall dad walk to the sidelines and stop near Mom. She didn't seem to notice him but began to pace up and down with Karin.

When the second quarter came, the coach pulled Karin over to the side and talked to her. Karin put on the long-sleeved goalie shirt. ''Oh, no,'' Mom's voice said. She was near me now—a bit in front, though, and didn't notice me sitting behind her. The game proceeded. ''I hate it when Karin's the goalie,'' Mom muttered to herself.

''She's a good goalie,'' said the tall man beside Mom. He seemed to be pacing up and down the line too.

''It makes me nervous,'' Mom said. ''I'm afraid she'll get kicked in the face.''

Karin pounced on the ball like a leopard. She waited for the other players to move out of the way, and then she stood and punted the ball. The game flowed to the other end of the field. Karin was alone.

"See, Mom?" said the man beside her.

She looked at him. He was tall and lean, and when he crunched on his candy bar, which he held like a half-peeled banana, dimples flashed in his cheeks. He smiled at her. "Karin's a tough kid in the goal."

I was pleased. This stranger had observed my sister's skill.

"I'm Dan Sanders," the stranger said to Mom. "My daughter is Jill, number six."

I saw Mom look at Jill, number six, who gave the ball a good kick that sent it back to Karin near our own goal.

"It makes me nervous when they kick it back to Karin like that," Mom said. "I'm afraid it'll slip out of her hands and score for the wrong team."

The man grinned. Karin picked up the ball and kicked it to a teammate, who dribbled it down the field. "Karin says you're not married or anything."

I sat up straight. Who was this bold guy, anyway? Had he been spying on us?

"That's right," Mom said.

"Me either."

Oh, no!

The man looked relaxed, and his wispy brown hair dangled in the breeze. He smiled at Mom-Jo again. "I don't beat around the bush," he said.

"I can see that," Mom answered.

"Would you have dinner with me tonight?"

I fell sideways to the ground.

"Well—I—" Mom stammered.

I needed to do something about this man right now! But what?

The man didn't let Mom finish stammering. "Before you answer, I need to tell you something—just so you'll know." He cleared his throat. "I always say this right away."

Mom waited.

"Most ladies aren't interested in me because there's something that, uh . . . scares them. So I like to flat out tell it for starters."

What? He was a criminal? A thief? No, a murderer. He'd murdered his wife. . . .

"I . . ." He cleared his throat again. "I have four children."

That was it? *That* was *it?*

Mom began to laugh, right out loud in the middle of a soccer game. She laughed while Karin blocked the ball with her knees and then dove on it. A player couldn't stop running, and she fell over Karin. They both rolled in the grass and then got up. I held my breath. Karin was okay. So was the other girl. Mom began to laugh again. And when she finished laughing, she sighed a big sigh.

The man was no longer beside her. He had moved down to the end of the field. There was a hurt look on his face and a slouch to his shoulders.

The game was over now, and the girls were cheering— our girls. They grabbed their drinks, listened to their coach tell them stuff they already knew, and went their separate ways. After sending Karin to the car, Mom followed the tall man to his van. I trotted along behind Mom so I could hear what she said to him.

After he helped his kid into the van, I heard him say, "Wait here." He came toward Mom.

"Come to my house for supper tonight," she said. I couldn't believe her boldness. Was *she* taking a bull by the horns? But wait—this man wasn't rich. Look at the junk inside his van: tennis shoes, a hammer, newspapers, a teddy bear with its arm missing. . . .

"You don't have to feel sorry for me," the man said. His words came out jaggedly from beneath his mustache. I was glad he wasn't going to accept.

"Come to my house at 6:30," Mom said. "I live at 1648 Orchard. Bring your kids."

His eyes quizzed hers. "What?"

"You heard me." She turned around and bumped right into me. "You nosy little bug," she muttered, and we walked to Karin and the car.

I worried all the way home. I worried because I didn't even know this stranger who would spend suppertime at our house. I worried because he might not like my mom. Then I worried because he might like her. I worried because I might like him, and he wouldn't like us. And I worried because I might not like him, and he might like us. I did a lot of worrying. I would've worried much less if he drove a Mercedes instead of an old van.

"What does the man in the gray van know about us?" Mom asked Karin as we turned the corner. Mom was probably worrying too.

"Nothin'."

"He knows I'm not married."

"That's 'cause he said, 'Karin, I never see your dad out here.' So I told him I just had you."

"I already forgot the guy's name. What is it?"

"I don't know."

"What's the daughter's name?"

"Jill something."

After much debating about what to feed the stranger and his kids, we decided to have chili and cold fruit salad, mainly because Mom had the ingredients in the house, and because it could feed a crowd easily. Lulu, Fred, and "Mr. Right" had probably just finished eating steak and strawberry cream cheese crepes. I didn't bring that up, though, because I didn't want Mom to feel bad. Here, instead of attending a lunch party that would've been served to her, she was fixing supper for ten people, and some of them she didn't even know. I call that getting the short end of the stick.

Chapter Three

Guess Who's Coming to Dinner?

We helped Mom clean the house, and then while she got dressed, George Washington and Karin baked their specialty, brownies. Mom tried on her mint green dress and white beads but said it felt too much like church. She should probably wear something that matched chili. She ended up changing into her gray outfit with the dusty rose sweater. "After all," she said, "this isn't a date. I'm cooking dinner for ten people."

"You look good," I told her. And she did. I was no longer worried. I was petrified.

While I was trying to make my hair lie down flat, Blake let our guests into the living room. I heard them come in. I heard George Washington offer them hot brownies. I heard Karin inform everyone that you don't serve brownies first, stupid. You serve them last. Then I heard Blake introduce himself—Blake Tooley—and George Washington and Karin Rogers and Samuel Rogers—that's me—as I entered the room.

"Why do you guys have so many different last names?" Jill asked.

"Because our dads had different last names," Blake offered politely.

By now Mom had reached the doorway.

"How many times has your mom been married, anyway?" Jill asked.

"Never been married at all," George Washington said proudly.

"She has, too," Blake argued.

"Huh?" George Washington responded. "To who?"

"Doug. Don't you remember Doug?"

"No. Doug who? Where is he now? Who's Doug?"

Karin took on the responsibility of answering the question. "She was *engaged* to Doug," she said in the know-it-all voice I hated. "He ran away."

The man on the couch was taking it all in. He saw Mom, and grinned. That's when I knew he wasn't going to escape out the door. He was quietly observing our household. And he was patiently listening to my little brothers and sister unfold the elements of Mom's life. He knew the story wasn't finished yet, and his eyes sparkled with something that looked like anticipation—and amusement.

"Hello," Mom said.

The man stood up and introduced us to his children, one by one: Jill, the oldest; Robin, the second—a girl with some plastic things in her ears; Natalie, a kindergartner; and a little kid named Emmie. I think she was probably a girl too, but she was wearing boy socks, and her shorts and shirt looked like they'd been wrestled in.

After the man finished introducing his kids, George Washington said, "I don't want to sit by the kid with the ear things."

We all ignored him.

We managed to assemble around the table, which had been lengthened with a card table that stretched from the dining room into the hall. Since I was Mom's right-hand man, I offered to give thanks. When I finished, the man and his kids all said, "Amen," and we began to eat.

Mom sat at one end of the long table, and the dad person, whose name nobody could remember, sat at the other. They reminded me of two silent bookends while the rest of us talked between them. We talked about school and friends. We discussed what kind of dog is the best (St. Bernard, because you could ride on its back) and who could probably burp the loudest in the world (King Kong).

Every once in a while Mom's eyes would meet the man's. He, I'm sure, was wondering how he got conned into visiting the house of a woman who had four children with different last names. I almost got the giggles once for no reason at all, but I was able to work 'em down toward my stomach where they finally dissolved.

Blake and the small kid named Natalie got everything straightened out for us. Natalie explained that her mom couldn't come today because she was in heaven. Blake said his was too, his real mom, and that Mom-Jo was his "acting mom," a term Lulu used. Blake went on to explain how Mom got us. Then he offered her mommying services to anyone who needed them. She was up for grabs.

The man looked relieved, or something. He spoke his first words of the meal. "That sounds like a nice idea, Blake—you sharing your mom," he said. "Where do I sign up?"

"You're too old," snapped George Washington.

The man ladled himself another bowl of chili and didn't speak again. I guess he'd been put in his place.

The table conversation became animated when the subject of soccer came up. Everyone participated except for the littlest girl, who sat wide-eyed near her daddy. George Washington and Natalie sat side by side, not aware of each other, yet both turning their heads in unison to follow the conversation.

"I've been playing soccer since I was a baby," said Karin's braggy voice.

"I've been playing since *before* I was a baby," said a challenging voice, Blake's, who'd played only once.

Everyone laughed.

I had given up on being embarrassed. It was too late.

Natalie's eyes narrowed. Kids' voices rattled on, yet her little head stopped turning. In fact, she did not move at all until there was a gap in the conversation. "So—" her high-pitched voice began. "Where *were* we before we were babies?"

A slight pause was followed by more conversation and then another pause.

"Where was I? Was I in heaven? Was I a kitten?" Natalie asked loudly.

A kitten?

"No," Jill answered. "You were a pickle."

Everyone laughed again.

Soccer stories turned to baseball stories, and we were wrapped up in tales of umps and RBIs.

During all of this Natalie seemed to be staring real hard into her chili bowl. Then she looked at Mom. "Excuse me, Mrs. Washington?" she said.

"Yes," Mom-Jo answered, even though her name isn't Mrs. Washington.

"What do you put in this lovely chili recipe?"

"Chili beans, tomato soup, and seasonings."

"Oh." Natalie stared down at her soup. Her spoon lay flat against the table. "Mrs. Washington?"

"Yes?"

"Do you put bugs in your chili?"

Mom seemed to flinch. "No. Why do you ask?"

"There's bugs in my chili."

"What?"

"Let me see this." The man pulled Natalie's bowl toward him so he could look into it. "I don't see any bugs."

"There." She pointed into the bowl. "Floating around. I saw one swimming a minute ago."

"Those aren't bugs. They're seasonings."

I looked down into my own soup, where little bits of seasonings floated in the broth.

"The seasonings move because you wiggle the bowl," the man said. He pushed the bowl back to her.

I decided maybe I was getting full of chili. I put my spoon down.

Natalie picked up her spoon and stirred the chili. "I'm sorry, everyone, but I have bugs in my chili."

"You do not," Karin said.

"Do too."

At that point Mom-Jo must have decided to take the bull by the horns. "Natalie," she said. "Let me see your bowl."

Natalie shoved her bowl at Mom, who scrutinized it very carefully, stirring and staring. "Oh, Natalie," she said. "You are so lucky! These are El Specialito Mexicano Chili Bugs! I haven't seen them in years! Oh, they're so delicious. Can I have this bowl—and you can have mine?"

"Sure."

Personally, I was so embarrassed about this whole supper that I wished I could put my face in my bowl with the chili bugs and drown to death.

Blake spoke. "Baby Ruth was an orphant."

The conversation rolled ahead. We moved from Babe Ruth to orphans to Orphan Annie and then to helicopters. Orphan Annie was rescued by a helicopter. Everyone paused to remember it.

Since Mom and Natalie had traded bowls, everyone was eating again.

Natalie was the first one done. ·

"Well," George Washington said. "Where are the brownies?"

I glanced at the dad. He had sort of grinned through the whole meal.

"Kid brownies on the back porch," Mom answered.

We cleared the table, grabbed brownies, and ran outside, but I came back in. Even though our new basketball hoop hung temptingly over the garage door, I decided to stay inside to work in the kitchen and keep an eye on things. Mom took the coffee pot and two cups down to Mr. Visitor's end of the table. The little girl had climbed up on his lap and wrapped her fingers around one of his shirt buttons; now she was sucking on her thumb.

"So," Mom said to the man. "Do you still think I pity you?" She poured them both a cup of coffee.

He closed his fingers around the handle of his cup. "No," he said. "I think you probably understand me better than anyone I know."

When they looked at each other, my stomach got tight. I threw a napkin at the kitchen trash. It missed, but I didn't care. I kicked it at the wall.

While Mom and the man sipped their coffee and ate their brownies, they seemed to savor the peace that had taken over the room. When I peeked at them, I felt as if I'd trampled through the woods and accidentally stumbled upon a beautiful snow scene; and now I didn't want to tussle it up with footprints, so I stayed in the kitchen.

"This house reminds me of my childhood home," I heard the man say.

"It belonged to my sister and her husband. I inherited it when I inherited the kids."

His chair creaked. "Our ceilings were high like this. Only there were cracks, and we tried to cover them with strategic slats of wood that ran across the borders and into the middle, crossing here and there. . . ."

If his family tried to cover up the ceiling cracks with boards, he must be poorer than a potato bug. I tossed more napkins into the trash and kicked the can.

"Would you like to see the rest of the house?" Mom asked.

No, Mom, I said in my heart. *Make him go away. He's not rich.*

"I'd like that," he said. I moved to the right so I could see him. He was lifting the little girl off his lap. "Emmie, why didn't you go use the potty?"

"Where is it?"

"Excuse us," he said to Mom.

I turned to the sink and pretended like I was working. I picked up a spoon and got squished chili on my thumb. Yuck. The man took Emmie out to the van, and she came back wearing different clothes. There was a wet spot on the man's pant leg. "This potty training business has me stumped," he said matter-of-factly to me as he walked by.

I couldn't think of an answer for him, and he went on through with Emmie trailing behind.

Mom gave him the house tour. She showed him the basement with its old coal bin, now stuffed with wood for the fireplace. She showed him the kitchen porch, and the pantry, and the downstairs bedrooms where Karin and I park all our favorite stuff.

When Mom was showing him the pictures on the piano, a bunch of us kids came and stood with them. Mom carefully explained which of her children belonged to each set of parents.

The dad turned to his kids. "Jill and Nat, do you need something?"

"No, Dad. We were just listening," Jill said.

"I would like you to take Emmie outside."

Jill and Natalie didn't look too thrilled about the idea, but they obeyed their dad.

I decided that I shouldn't leave Mom alone in the presence of a stranger, so I followed them upstairs where she showed him our homemade art gallery in the hall and then the upstairs bedrooms. Last they went into her own room, which had a light table in the corner and a door to the balcony over the porch roof. She had been sketching skunks, and they were spread out all over the wide wood and glass table. "I'm trying to work up a hat emblem for a baseball team called 'Sutter's Skunks,' " she said.

The man walked over to the table. "I like this one." He pointed to the last one she had drawn. "Who are these drawings for?"

"Western Hats and Tees."

He paused. "I think I've worn your artwork on my head. Puffy's Pet Products—with the cat?"

"I did that one."

I wondered why a grown man would wear a hat that said "Puffy's Pet Products."

They talked of T-shirts and screen printing and team logos for a while, and then Mom opened the door to the balcony. They went out together and sat down on the bench Mom and I had placed there last summer.

"I'll show you how this works," Mom said to him. She scrunched down in her seat and propped her feet up on the balcony rail. He did the same. Since the man was in *my* seat, I sat on the floor beside Mom. For some reason, I wanted to be tight by her side. She seemed to sense it and did not ask me to leave, probably because I'm her right-hand man.

We heard the basketball bouncing off things: the hoop, the garage door, the roof, our car. The sun was dipping below the red-tinged trees. No one spoke right away. We just soaked up the sights and sounds around us. My mind wandered to the noises below. A little voice cried, and the basketball stopped bouncing. The crying stopped, and the basketball started up again. Was it Emmie who had cried?

"Emmie must be okay," the man said.

"I'd say so. Karin would report to me if she wasn't," Mom said.

I sniffed. Then I decided to stay quiet. I should probably go downstairs with the other kids. Besides, this was boring. I slipped back into the house but stopped by the light table and turned around.

Mom and the man were talking seriously, silhouetted against the orange sky with their faces pointed at each other. How different they were from the kids who usually bounced on Mom's balcony bench! Karin and I usually pushed each other back and forth, and Blake and George Washington liked to throw their toys off the balcony. Once we caught them tossing all their money into the grass below. They said they were being kind kings.

Mom-Jo and the guy didn't move at all, except for their mouths. They probably could've sat there for hours and hours and hours without getting tired because they weren't using any energy—until he stood up.

He stood and turned toward Mom-Jo. He put one foot on the bench and rolled his pant leg up to his knee. Judging by the look on Mom's face, this guy had the ugliest leg in town. He patted his stomach before he fixed the pant cuff back and sat down. Then they went back to their lazy talking position. I decided it was time to go play with the kids. Perhaps a little basketball shooting would calm my nerves.

After the man and his kids left, I helped Mom finish doing the dishes. Actually, I don't like cleanup work, but I did want a chance to talk to Mom. She was putting the good dishes up high. I walked up beside her and handed 'em to her so she wouldn't have to keep reaching up and down. In a matter of minutes we had everything put up square.

"Mom," I said to her as she took off her apron.

"Yes, dear."

"Did you tell Jill's dad the sentence I can't hear until I'm sixteen?"

"Nineteen. Good try."

"Did you say the sentence?"

"No."

"Why not?"

"He said it first." She smiled and then chuckled a bit.

I tried to remember Jill's dad saying anything that would make my mom laugh, but nothing came to mind right away.

It didn't hit me until I put my head down on my pillow. I closed my eyes and remembered Karin's soccer game today. She'd played well. So had Jill. I remembered the tall man standing beside Mom. I remembered him saying that there was some information he needed to tell her right off the bat, something that put dread in me until I heard it. In my mind I heard the sentence, "I have four children." And I heard Mom laugh.

What was so funny about having four children? Nothing. What was so funny about a man offering his information before Mom could give hers?

I have four children?

My stomach hurt and my head hurt. I couldn't sleep. I sat up in my bed. No good thoughts could come to me now.

I remembered Mom and the man talking to each other after dinner, and the words, "I think you understand me better than anyone I know." My fingers twitched against the covers.

I walked to my door and looked up the stairs. Mom's light was still on; she must be working on skunks.

I was right. I stood on her left side so I wouldn't get in the way of her drawing arm. She was using the glass part of the table so she could trace her own work on regular white paper. Neither of us spoke until she finished coloring in the tail.

"Mom."

"Yes, dear."

"I know the sentence you say." She placed her pen in the rack.

"It's 'I have four children.' Isn't it?"

She put her arms around me. "Yes, it is."

I almost started to cry. I was one of the reasons why pretty Mom-Jo had no husband. I blinked hard.

"Samuel." She held me close against her so I couldn't see her face. "I love my four children. You are worth it— each one of you. Don't forget." She kissed me on the forehead.

"Jill's dad knows you have four kids, and he didn't run away," I said.

"You're right, dear."

"Good night, Mom."

"Good night."

Things would never be the same again. A man was going to be mixed up in our life—this week, anyway. But that wasn't my major concern.

These words were my major concern: *I have four children*. I wondered if those words had driven Doug away. I wondered if they would keep Mom-Jo from ever having a boyfriend or getting married. Words that scared men away. I hated the words. I wished I hadn't heard them 'til I was nineteen.

Chapter Four

Mr. Appadoosa

The next Wednesday a strange thing happened. I was sitting in the kitchen doing my homework when I heard a knock at the front door. Nobody uses our front door except the mailman—and strangers.

Since Mom was upstairs drawing and the kids were out back, I went to the door and opened it. Jill's dad was standing on the porch with a big wad of money in his hand: green dollar bills. He looked surprised to see me.

"I thought you'd be in school," he said.

"We got out early today so Mom could take us to the dentist. Only, the dentist had an emergency, so we came home."

"Lucky you."

I felt George Washington worm his way between me and the doorpost. "Where's the kid with the ear things?" he asked.

"Robin?"

"Yeah. Where is she?"

"At school."

"Kids with ear things go to school?"

"Yes, sir."

"Oh."

Jill's dad seemed to be staring past us into the room. There was no one there, of course. Mom was upstairs. "Is your mom here?"

"Yes." I turned to George Washington and told him to go get Mom. Then I faced Jill's dad again. "Would you like to come in?"

"Yes," he said as he stepped inside. While we waited for Mom he stuffed the money wad into his shirt pocket. I noticed there were black smudges all over the ends of his fingers.

When I heard Mom's footsteps behind me, the man's face broke into a grin that worked itself clear up into his eyes. I didn't want him to be that happy to see Mom. He held the dollar bills out for her to take. "Here's the money in case you want to get an early start," he said.

"Okay." She took it from him. I was surprised she didn't thank him for it. She's usually so polite. She told me to go back and finish my math, so I left. Before I got all the way into the kitchen I looked over my shoulder and saw the man saying something to Mom while she wrote on a piece of paper. Pretty soon he left, and Mom went upstairs.

I looked down at my book. I really didn't care about fractions right now. I wanted to know about the money. Why did Jill's dad give it to Mom? Why hadn't she thanked him for it? What did he want, anyway?

Mom's feet padded down the stairs again. "I'm going to run these drawings over to Lulu," she said to me. "Keep an eye on the kids. I'll be right back. Oh—and don't forget to empty the wastebaskets. Tomorrow is trash day, you know."

Mom always remembers trash day, and I always take care of wastebasket duty. Once I asked Blake and George Washington to do it for me. Blake stood at the top of the stairs, and George stood at the bottom with an open grocery bag in his hands. "Bombs away!" Blake said. I walked into the hall just as Blake dumped Mom's wastebasket over the edge of the banister. I think the trash was supposed to land in George Washington's sack, but it didn't. Envelopes fluttered like leaves on crooked air paths, crumpled papers scattered like bombs, and an ink bottle broke on the new tile. Now, every time I walk past the stain, I remember that day and the unhappiness it caused Mom. This is what I thought of as I trudged up the stairs.

The kids were out playing backy-ball. Since Blake and George Washington were too weak and silly to make real baskets in the hoop, Karin and I invented backy-ball for them. Instead of aiming at the hoop, we aim at each others' backs. If we hit the other guy, we get points. If somebody cries, all his points go away.

I looked down at the light table while I bent to pick up the wastebasket. There was money tucked neatly in the open drawer. I took it out and counted it—three hundred dollars in twenty dollar bills. I stared at it. A man we barely knew had handed this thick wad of cash to my mom. What if he was involving her in some sort of scam? What should I do? I put the money back in the drawer.

I would need to keep a close watch on Mom. She needed a protector, and I was all she had.

All my hopes were dashed when we pulled into Jill's driveway. I'd really hoped she would be rich, especially after her dad had given Mom the three hundred dollars. I'd even prayed that she would be rich, and that her dad would marry Mom and buy us a new car because the one we were in right now had rattled all the way to Jill's house. We bumped down Jill's gravel driveway and stopped beside their van, which looked as ugly as a toad.

Everything was old: the house, the little barn, the empty rabbit cages alongside the garage. Even the swing hanging from the big old tree branch was worn down. George Washington raced to the swing and sat on it. "Push me!" he yelled. Nobody answered. Karin, Blake, and I followed Mom up the porch steps.

"Welcome to the Taj Mahal," Jill's dad said to Mom as he opened the screen door.

Mom laughed. I have no idea why.

The huge room we entered was full of everything in the world, from folded laundry against the wall, to two cats and the kid, Robin, asleep on the couch, to newspapers and doll clothes.

"Jill's upstairs," the man said to Karin.

Karin disappeared up the stairs before I could even figure out where they were. My eyes were still hopping around the room trying to find a point to settle on. Besides the two cats, I saw a cocker spaniel, and a turtle in a goldfish bowl. I did stare for a couple of minutes at the little basketball hoop stuck to the top of a door and then at a pile of tennis balls sitting in a chair like eggs in a nest.

"My goodness," Blake said. I noticed he had his hands on his hips. "This place is atrocious!" His voice sounded just like Mom's did when she looked at our rooms. "Ain't it, Mom? Look over there!" He pointed to a pile of news-papers and doll clothes beside the couch.

Mom looked kind of embarrassed.

Jill's dad smiled and picked up Emmie, who stood be-side him. He pointed to the car seat that was sitting in the corner. "Sam," he said to me. "Do you think you can get that?"

I picked it up and followed him and Mom back out to her car. Then the dad stuck the car seat into Mom's car and showed her how to stick Emmie in it. Of course, Mom already knew how to do car seats because Blake and George Washington used to sit in 'em, but Mom just watched the guy show her anyway. That's how Mom is around grown-ups, sort of the opposite of bossy. The guy gave Emmie a big kiss on the cheek and said, "Have a good time." Mom got in behind the wheel. "You have a good time too," he told her.

"I will," she said, and off they went.

"Where are they going?" Blake asked him.

"Shopping. Girl stuff," the man answered. "I'm no good at shopping."

I noticed that the little kid, Natalie, had joined George Washington at the swing. Blake ran to play with them. I didn't know what I was supposed to do, so I turned to Jill's dad, who seemed awful tall up this close. "You got a TV?" I asked him.

"Well, it broke and we haven't fixed it yet."

Boy, I thought, they must really be poor.

"Follow me," he said.

We went back in through the junky living room to the back of the house. The kitchen was cluttered too, but it smelled okay, and most of the clutter was papers and toys. The food had been wiped up and put away—or maybe they didn't have any food. Maybe the dad had given away all his money to Mom for a shopping spree, and he didn't have any left for food.

"I have work to do," he said as he pushed against a door. He set a brick by the door to keep it open, and he turned on a light.

There were all kinds of typewriters in the room, and most of them were taken apart. There were trays of tools here and there. It looked like the living room did, only it had a theme: typewriters. The man put on a long blue apron that tied behind his back.

I still didn't know what I was supposed to do, especially with no TV, so I decided to think up my own entertainment. "You want me to clean your living room?" I asked him. Then I felt embarrassed because maybe he didn't realize what a mess it was.

He put on his glasses, which were lopsided, and he faced me. "Sure," he said. "I'll pay you a buck."

I felt terrible. He was the poor person, and he was going to pay me a buck? I decided I would accept the money, because Mom said that sometimes it makes poor people feel good if they can give you something. Later, I could sneak it back into the man's cookie jar so he could buy some rice for supper.

I felt as if I was in charge, just like when I'm at home. I could hear Karin and Jill upstairs playing school with stuffed animals. The three little kids seemed happy outside, and I was glad to have them out of my hair. Robin looked like she was dead, but I know she wasn't because dead people don't drool. I wondered why she wore those plastic things in her ears the day she came to our house. There was nothing in her ears now. The two cats still slept quietly against her leg.

"Do you need anything, Sam?" a voice behind me said.

"Oh, no." I turned around. I didn't want him to catch me staring at his kid like that.

"These cats always follow my Robin around," he said. "She's gentle natured, and they like that." The man scratched one of the cats under the chin. "Are you wondering about Robin?"

"Huh?"

"Are you wondering about her ears?"

I shrugged.

"Robin wears hearing aids in both ears. Usually her hair covers them up, but sooner or later you notice."

"Where are they now?"

He grinned. "She takes them out when she doesn't want to hear me. She broke a bowl in the kitchen and ran in here. I followed her to talk to her, and she was lying right here on the couch with her eyes shut. Her hearing aids were not in her ears, as you've noticed. I decided to let her be alone for a while to cool down. She fell asleep. Eventually, she'll wake up and need her 'ears' back. Then we'll talk."

"What do I do if I find 'em when I'm cleaning?"

"I already found them. They're in my pocket."

"Oh."

"Just don't bump her when you're working. It'll startle her."

"I'll keep my distance."

The man pointed to the door with the hoop on it. "The vacuum sweeper is in there."

"Thanks."

He left.

There were a lot of things I wasn't sure about. I didn't know where to put the tennis balls, or the newspapers, or the doll clothes, or anything. So I just arranged it all in a neat pile next to the couch. Then I dusted with an undershirt I found on the steps, and I vacuumed the rug, which woke up the cats. As they stretched and moved about, Robin woke too. I decided that the cats were a nice, soft type of alarm clock system for the little deaf girl. When she opened her eyes and stared at me, I waved. That seemed to make her fears go away, for she sat up and looked around the room. Then she began to hunt. She looked between the couch cushions first and then under the newspapers I'd just stacked. "Ears?" she said to me.

I pointed to the typewriter room and said, "Dad."

She left.

When I had finished my job, I went back to the typewriter room. The man was working alone, all bent over a typewriter. His face was almost pressed against the machine, and he looked frustrated.

"I'm done," I said.

"Good. Go get a Pepsi out of the refrigerator."

"Aren't you going to check my work?"

"I trust you." He was trying to fit a skinny little screwdriver between two wires. I waited while he worked on it.

"When's my mom coming back?" I asked.

"Not for a couple hours."

"I don't know what I should do next." Clean the whole house? Yuck.

He set the screwdriver down. "I need to get away from this." He sighed. "Let's take the kids fishing."

"Girls? And little kids?"

He took off his glasses and rubbed his eyes. "Why not?"

"I don't know." If he wanted to take a bunch of girls and little kids fishing, that was his business. I suppose I wouldn't mind going along.

I'd been fishing several times with Mike and his dad, but my sister and brothers had never been. Mom avoids fishing because she doesn't like to do stuff that smells bad.

Jill's house was set up for fishing. We got bait out of the refrigerator (right between the Jell-O and leftover spaghetti). We grabbed cane poles off the back porch, and we walked down a path through tall trees to a rock ledge along a clear, shallow stream.

If Mom had been there, she would've lined us up and said, "Don't get wet, don't touch anything dirty," and so on. But Mr. Whatever-his-name-was didn't say anything like that. He said, "Don't flick your hook up in the air where it might land in a tree branch—or worse, in your eye."

He gave Karin and Jill and me the three poles with hooks on the ends. We got busy sticking on the bait—little ugly worms. I was surprised at how easily Jill fixed her hook, like she'd done it a million times before. Karin, who would never act like a sissy, gritted her teeth and took care of hers too, while I did mine. I noticed that the little kids all got poles with rubber worms tied to the ends of the fishing lines. I guess Jill's dad didn't trust them yet.

One by one the little kids got tired of fishing and handed their poles to Jill's dad, who laid them in a row. I tried real hard to catch a fish so Jill's dad could have a supper for his family, but no bites touched my line, or Karin's, or Jill's.

Blake saw the toads first, and soon we all had put down our poles so we could catch them. Jill's dad was the fastest toad catcher I ever saw.

Even though the water was ice cold, I managed to catch the biggest toad I could find. I named him Kerm. We all caught toads and put them into the bucket we'd carried out to load up with fish.

When we got back to the house, Jill's dad made us take off our shoes and socks on the big back porch. He sent Jill and Karin into the house to find some dry clothes for themselves, and then he stripped everyone that was left down to the underwear. I helped him put all the muddy clothes into the washer in the kitchen, and then we added our own shirts. I decided my shorts would be okay. He had a big mud blob on the back of his, so he took 'em off and threw 'em in. He was wearing striped gym shorts underneath, so it didn't matter.

What did matter were the huge scars that ran jaggedly along his belt line and down his leg. When he saw me notice the biggest one, which ran along his stomach like an ugly twig-shaped bump, he pulled his waistband up to cover it. That made him look like a skinny version of Humpty Dumpty in striped shorts.

We went back to the porch, where the little kids were playing with toads. Jill's dad took a piece of chalk and drew a line at one end of the porch, which was as long as the house. "Bring me those toads," he said to Jill, who had returned with Karin. They carried the bucket down to where he was.

Even though he stood tall and cleared his throat in a very professional manner, his high-water shorts and mud-spattered glasses killed any ideas about this being a serious adventure. Still, the kids all waited reverently for him to make his statement. "I'm here to announce that my toad, Mr. Appadoosa, is the best long jumper in the state." Jill's dad reached into the bucket and pulled out a fat, plain looking little dude, and set him behind the chalk line. "I challenge anyone to beat Mr. Appadoosa in a jumping contest." Mr. Appadoosa sat like a statue.

"Is he alive?" Jill asked. I wondered that myself.

"Yes," answered the man. He got down on his knees behind the toad. "I'll show you how it's done. All toads are allowed three hops. The longest jumper wins."

"Wins what?" Blake asked.

The man rubbed his chin and looked at me. "What do you think?" he asked me.

What kind of a prize can a poor man provide for kids? I tried to think fast. Something cheap—or better yet, free. I reached into my pocket and felt around: a steely marble, some tissue, Mike's polished agate. . . . I pulled out the marble. "This?" Immediately, I regretted what I had done. This marble was from my famous old collection. I'd passed most of 'em on down to Blake. But this one, the steely, I'd kept because it was my favorite, gray and smooth, with the heavy feel that makes steelies feel different from regular glass marbles. Jill's dad was eyeing the marble.

"Nice prize, Sam."

"That's real pretty, Sam," Jill said.

I'd hoped none of the little kids would want my marble, but I could tell by the hungry looks on their faces that it was a fine prize, so I set it on the windowsill for everyone to see.

The man put his face near his dead-looking toad and spoke. "Mr. Appadoosa, my honor is at stake. Do your most athletic work." Then he smacked the floor hard with his hand. Everyone jumped. Mr. Appadoosa sat like a rock.

Jill began to laugh, so the rest of us did too. Her dad looked so funny with his blotty glasses and silly shorts, and his hair all sticking out like chicken feathers while he crouched over a stupid toad. He sat up on his knees. "Mr. Appadoosa has decided that he does not need to practice. Now he will perform."

We all held our breath while the man prepared to give the floor his next slap. Just as he raised his hand, my eye caught a movement from beside the house. Then he dove downward and slapped the floor with all his might. SMACK, SMACK, SMACK! We all jumped, including Mr. Appadoosa, who ended up right at Mom's feet. She and Emmie stood at the edge of the porch with their mouths open.

Jill's dad got up real fast, and his face turned red clear up to his ears. "Excuse me, ma'am," he said while he tugged at the waist of his shorts. He looked at me, said, "Sam, take care of my champion toad," and ran into the house. I carefully picked up Mr. Appadoosa and put him in the bucket with the others.

While we waited for Jill's dad to come back out, none of us could get our toads to jump as far as Mr. Appadoosa had. Then we tried Mr. Appadoosa. He wouldn't jump for us either; he sat like a stone. Jill picked up my precious marble and said she would give it to her dad, and she went into the house. I wished I'd chosen the agate instead.

It took three trips for Mom to get all the packages out of the car. She and Emmie had bought all kinds of girl clothes for Jill and her sisters. Mom said they would be stocked up for a long time. When Jill's dad came downstairs in his normal clothes, with his hair combed and the mud-blobs off his glasses, Mom had the girls try on some of their new outfits for his approval. He seemed real pleased and told her he had never seen anybody who could stretch three hundred dollars that far. I felt ashamed about snooping at the money in Mom's drawer, but I didn't tell anyone.

Jill's dad told Mom to go home and get ready while he took all of us out to McDonald's. I didn't really want him to spend all his money on us, but he insisted. When he got there he acted kind of surprised when Karin and I ordered water to drink. Then George Washington ordered a large Coke. Karin and I both kicked him at the same time, so he changed his order to water. I told Jill's dad to make his kids have water, too, because it saves money. He told us to go sit down.

When we got settled, he carried our food over, and the last tray was full of Cokes. He set one in front of each of us. Then he bowed his head. "Gracious Lord," he said clearly, "thank You for each precious kid at this table. Be with the evening ahead. Keep us all in Your protective care. In Jesus' name, Amen."

"Dad," Natalie said. "You forgot the food again."

"Oh, yeah." He shut his eyes. "Thank You for the food."

His kids all said, "Amen," in unison.

Everyone smiled, probably because of the wonderful drinks we all had. We drank.

He didn't buy anything for himself. I wondered if our Cokes took up all the money he needed for his part of the supper.

He dropped his kids off at their grandma's house, then he took us home. Mom was waiting in the living room, and she was dressed real pretty. She sent Karin upstairs to run a bath for George Washington and Blake. She sent the two little guys to get into their pajamas.

Mom told me I was in charge. She gave me the phone number of the restaurant she and Jill's dad were going to, which was close by. Now I understood why he didn't eat at McDonald's.

Jill's dad took Mom's arm and walked her out the front door. I felt like he was taking over our lives, and I decided I didn't like it, even though he had taken us fishing, and to the toad olympics, and to McDonald's for supper and a Coke.

Something clunked on the front porch, so I looked out. Jill's dad had just set the toad bucket by the steps. "Kerm'll be okay here for now, Sam," he said. "But I'd let him go in the morning—out back somewhere. Let him eat the bugs under your cool bushes."

"Okay."

"Lock up the house real tight."

"I will."

"Sam?"

"Yeah."

He looked right at my face. "I'll have your mom home at a decent hour. I'll be good to her."

"Okay."

"Here's your dollar for cleaning the living room."

"No," I said. "You keep it. Use it for Mom's supper. She eats a lot."

He grinned and slid the dollar into his pocket. "She'll like that," he said as he walked toward the van.

I didn't have any trouble getting the kids settled in their beds because they were so tired from catching toads. I was tired too, and I couldn't even stay awake 'til Mom got home. I just remember her giving me a good-night kiss in the middle of my dream about Mr. Appadoosa taking over my life.

Chapter Five
Two Orphans

We saw quite a bit of Jill's dad after that. He took Mom to restaurants and plays, and racquetball, and Sunday night church. Even though his house and van stayed old-looking, he always had money to use on Mom. And he always insisted on paying me to babysit when he took her out. And he always talked to me before they went anywhere so I would know he would bring her home at a decent hour, and that he would be good to her.

I kind of liked to go to his house because we could play with the cats and dog, or catch toads, or do other stuff different from our house. But, as the months rolled by, I didn't like him being around so much and taking Mom away from me all the time. And—I wished he was rich.

Then came the day that we saw the three men in the grocery store. I was with Mom-Jo, being her right-hand man, and it was terrific since Karin was with Jill at her grandma's, and the boys were at an Awana Olympics practice. I had Mom-Jo all to myself for a change, except for the three men.

First, we saw Mike Banner's dad. He invited me to the father-son overnighter again. Mom said, "That would be so nice. Thank you, Ted," before I could open my mouth to speak.

He was gone in a jiffy, but I wanted to scream. I took a deep breath instead. "I hate going to the overnighter with Mr. Banner, Mom," I said. "He's the only guy that takes an extra kid. It makes me feel like I'm . . . Hobo Junior."

"He's just trying to be kind, Sam. His heart is in the right place." She sighed. "Besides, it'll give you a chance to be in a male-oriented environment for a change. Hiking, camping, fishing. Your dad used to love all those things, and I feel bad that you don't get to do them more often."

Hiking, camping, fishing . . . what about the campfire? I always hated the campfire part of the father-son over-nighter. Each dad got up and said something good about his son, and I always got left out because I wasn't really any-body's son.

"Sam, could you go back to the dairy section and get another gallon of milk?"

"Sure."

I stood and stared at the milk jugs, trying to figure out which one to take. The two per cent at our usual store had a pink lid. Here, none of them had pink lids, so I had to study the writing on their labels.

"You look grouchy," said a voice behind me.

I turned around to see Jill's dad. "Oh, hi," I said. His cart was loaded up with cereal and boxed macaroni. I don't think he cooked too great. "I feel grouchy," I said.

"Reading milk labels makes you grouchy?"

"No." I turned toward the milk and grabbed one with a green lid. I didn't bother to read it. Mom would tell me if it was the right one.

"So, why are you so grouchy?"

"I don't want to go to the father-son overnighter with Mike Banner and his dad again."

"That sounds like fun."

"It stinks."

I carried my milk off toward Mom-Jo.

I found her at the end of a long aisle containing canned goods. She was standing still, staring at two people who stood at the far end of the same aisle.

"What are you doing?" I asked.

"Nothing." She put the milk in the cart.

"Don't we know that guy?" I asked.

She put her arm around me. "It's Doug," she said. There was something settled and sad about the way she stood beside me, sort of like a prize fighter when he knows he lost and he can't do anything about it.

"Who's the lady?"

"His wife."

"Oh, sick."

Mom turned the basket away and took us to another aisle, the one with cake mixes. I knew she still needed to get some corn and peaches, but she probably didn't want to be in the same aisle with Doug and his wife. So we stood and stared at cake mixes. She asked me to choose one. I don't think she had the heart to think about cake and stuff right then, so I picked out her favorite, strawberry. Maybe I would bake it for her tonight, just to cheer her up.

Mike Banner's dad left long before we were finished, and somehow, we managed not to bump into Jill's dad at all. But Doug appeared here and there all over the store, and we sort of drove in circles to avoid him. Finally, he left too.

When we were waiting for our groceries to be checked out, I decided that men had done nothing good for Mom-Jo in her life or me in mine. We were better off without them, all of them.

"Let's see," Mom said as she checked off my list. "Sleeping bag, extra socks, underwear . . ."

I wasn't paying attention to her words. I wished I didn't have to go.

". . . fishing pole. This one Dan loaned you looks like a dandy. Sweatshirt, gum . . ."

I could hear a car stop in the driveway. Mike and his dad.

Jill's dad appeared on the porch, and his kids marched right along with him. He opened the door and let them all in. They were carrying purses, and teddy bears, and a potty chair. "Mine," Emmie said as she pointed to it proudly. Mom took it to the kitchen.

"Hey, that goes in the bathroom!" Natalie said.

"No, miss," Mom answered her. "It'll go in the kitchen, where the action is. Lots of drinking; lots of pottying."

"Emmie's going to stay here and do potty training in our kitchen?" I asked.

"We're all staying here," Jill said as she set a paper bag full of clothes on the floor. "This is my suitcase. We ran out of real ones."

Jill's dad picked up my gear and turned toward the door. "Go kiss your Mom good-bye," he said matter-of-factly. "I'm taking you to the father-son thing. You don't have a father. I don't have a son. We'll be orphans together."

I kissed Mom. Jill's dad kissed all his little girls, and then he kissed Mom—on the cheek—with everyone watching. I decided I would rather go with Mr. Banner than have Jill's dad kiss Mom, but I kept quiet. My fingers twitched and my stomach hurt all the way to the car.

It was nice not to share a dad, and I think Mike was glad to have his dad to himself for once.

When it was time for the campfire, I whispered to Jill's dad that we should go do something else for a while because the other guys were going to talk about their real sons. He said, "No way. I've never been to a father-son thing, and I want to do it one hundred per cent."

First, a man from our church read a Bible verse from Proverbs that said, *Hear, ye children, the instruction of a father, and attend to know understanding.* I was glad I didn't have a father to tell me what to do.

Then the guy read another verse: *Behold, what manner of love the Father hath bestowed upon us, that we should be called the sons of God.* I guess the guy was trying to remind us of God's love being like a father's love, or something. I pushed it all out of my mind. When I thought about having no father to love me, I felt sad. When I thought about having no father to boss me around, I felt okay. So, why should I be confused by thinking about stuff that didn't really happen to me anyway?

Besides, why was the bald man across the campfire staring at Jill's dad so hard? As the church guy continued to talk, the bald man continued to stare. I looked at Jill's dad myself and whispered to him, "Did you know there's a guy staring at you?"

"Yes," he whispered back.

"Why?"

"I don't know."

"Do you know him?"

"Maybe." Jill's dad looked back at the speaker, so I did too.

Then the speaker sat down. "Here it comes," I said to Jill's dad.

One by one the fathers stood up and said nice things about their sons. You could tell they'd thought about it a long time, each one trying to outdo the last one, talking about accomplishments and stuff. Mike's dad stood and said his usual talk about Mike being so honest and thoughtful. He was right. Mike is those things. I suppose his dad should be proud of him. I'd never really felt good about Mr. Banner's speech before since I was always so unhappy about being Hobo Junior. Tonight, the pressure was off.

I was real surprised when Jill's dad stood up. I tried to grab his pant leg to make him sit down, but he'd shot up so quick I couldn't do anything. "I'm here with Sam tonight because, as you know, his dad died in a plane crash five years ago." Everyone sure was quiet all of a sudden. "If Sam's dad could be here tonight to speak, he would probably say he was real proud of his son because of his good grades, his basketball talent, the fine example he sets for his little sister and brothers, and the way he handles his responsibility as man of the house." Jill's dad sat down.

It was quiet for a few long minutes while I fought tears that were trying to crowd out of my eyes. I did some hard blinking. Then another dad got up and started to talk about his kid. I was relieved that everyone was looking at him now instead of at us. I didn't dare look at Jill's dad. I couldn't believe he had just said all that stuff about me. I wondered if my real dad would've said those words. I wondered if he knew in heaven what kind of a kid I was now. I knew he used to like me when I was little. Would he like me now? According to Jill's dad—yes.

I quietly slipped away from the campfire. I found a spot past our tent where no one could see me, and I cried, just a little bit. Then I stood up straight, took a deep breath, and returned to my spot beside Jill's dad.

This was probably the worst campfire I'd ever attended in all the years I'd been coming to the overnighter. It was also, by far, the best.

"You don't have to call me Mr. Sanders all the time," Jill's dad told me. We were making sure all our gear was ready for the morning hike to the fishing hole. "You can call me Dan. That's probably easier. Don't you think?"

"Okay." I would try. It would feel strange to call him Dan, but also grown-up, like we were friends instead of a dad helping someone else's kid.

"Doc, how are you doing?" A voice interrupted us. The man who spoke from behind me was reaching his hand toward Jill's dad.

Jill's dad rose slowly and shook the man's hand. "Fine," he said. The man was the bald guy who'd stared across the campfire.

"We wondered what happened to you after the accident," the man said when their hands had parted.

"I needed a change," Jill's dad said. "I bought a quiet old place near here so I could raise the kids and sort out my thoughts."

"You look good, Doc."

Jill's dad grinned. "Thanks. I'm thinking that in a year or so I'll hang out my shingle again."

The man looked thoughtful for a moment. "Our family still prays for you."

"I appreciate your prayers."

The man didn't stay for long, probably because Jill's dad wasn't being real talkative just now.

I'd never slept in a tent with a stranger before. Jill's dad was so long his head touched the tent zipper and his feet touched the canvas at the other end, so he curled up his knees until they poked me through my sleeping bag.

"Sorry, Sam," he said while he unfolded his legs a bit. "This tent's not my size." He finally settled down, and his breathing became even.

I couldn't go to sleep. My eyes wouldn't shut, even though it was pretty dark around me. And my mind wouldn't turn off. First, I thought about the words Jill's dad had said at the campfire. I'd already memorized them, and they felt good inside of me, sort of like touching polished furniture. Then I wondered why the man who stared at Jill's dad had called him "Doc." I reached under my pillow for the folded up knife Jill's dad was letting me borrow. It was made of steel, smooth and glossy, and exactly the right fit for my palm.

"What are you doing?" he asked. I guess he couldn't sleep either.

"Checking the knife." I pressed it against my cheek. I heard him sigh. "Mr. Sanders?"

"Dan."

"Why did that man call you 'Doc'?"

"I'm a veterinarian."

He was? Then why did he fix typewriters in the back of his house?

"I *was* a veterinarian."

"What happened?"

"When Martha died, I had a hard time keeping up with four little girls and the animal clinic. I couldn't find anyone suitable to take care of the kids while I worked. So I took a day off work and spent the time in the woods with my Bible. I read and prayed. I gave the problem to God."

I remembered giving a problem to God: Mom-Jo's husband situation.

Mr. Sanders's arm brushed against the side of the tent. "I came back with a plan."

"What was the plan?"

"I sold my partnership in the clinic and put the money into a three-year, high-interest savings account. Then I stored my equipment and moved to the country. I went back to the trade that got me through college—typewriter repair—which I can do at home and still be with the kids." He paused for a minute. "I want them to be raised with strong Christian values. Martha and I both felt that was important." He stretched out 'til his feet pressed against the tent bottom, and then he scrunched up again. "Anyway, after the accident, I needed to, uh, recover, without all my friends and neighbors watching. I needed to be away."

"Will you be a vet again?" I asked.

"In time. I'm beginning to get the itch. I'll start slow; convert my barn into a clinic, I think. My money will be free soon."

"Vets are usually rich, aren't they?" My spirits lifted. Maybe he was the right man for Mom after all.

"Not vets who start from scratch and have four kids to support."

Four kids. He was hindered by four kids. I wished he hadn't mentioned that.

He sat up and unzipped his sleeping bag. Then he reached for the tent door. He fumbled for the zipper, found it, and unzipped it halfway. Then he turned his body around so his feet stuck out the flaps, and his head rested down at the other end of the tent.

"So Martha was your wife?" I asked him.

"Yes."

"How did she die?"

"Car accident. A drunk driver hit us."

"That's how you got those scars?"

"Yes."

What a terrible experience. He'd been in an accident, and it killed his wife. I took a deep breath before I asked him the next question that had been pressing on my mind. "Do you still miss her?"

"Part of me will always miss her." His voice came from the other end of the tent now, since his feet were out the door.

I spoke to his ankles. "What was she like?"

He was quiet for such a long time, I thought he had gone to sleep. As my eyes began to close, he sat up, and I jerked awake. He fumbled along the edge of the tent. I heard him find something, perhaps his socks? Yes, he was putting them on his feet. He lay down again and pushed his feet outside. "Martha was my best friend," he said.

"A *girl* was your best friend?"

He began to chuckle, then he stopped himself. But I wondered if deep inside he was still laughing, because I could feel his elbow tremble against my leg. Eventually, he sighed. "Are you still awake, Sam?"

"Yes."

"Who's your best friend?"

Mike was kind of a pain sometimes, so I said, "Mom-Jo."

"See? Your best friend is a girl."

"I never thought of it that way before." Good grief! Mom-Jo was my mom!

"What is Mom-Jo to you?" I asked him. We might as well get all these questions over and done with.

"She's someone I can talk to."

"What does that mean?"

"We understand each other. I care about her."

"Do you ever kiss her on the mouth?"

He was silent.

"Yes, then. Right?" I snapped. My stomach was all bunched up, and my fingers got twitchy. "Why do you kiss her?"

He didn't answer, but I felt sure he was smiling into the darkness.

For months I'd hoped for a man to meet Mom, and now that he had appeared, I wished he would go away. I sat up.

How could I sleep in the same tent with a man who'd kissed Mom-Jo? "I'm her right-hand man," I said firmly.

"I know."

"I'm her protector. Don't you ever forget." I couldn't believe I was actually saying those angry words to a grown-up.

He sat up, too, and we faced each other in the dark tent. I couldn't see his face, but I could tell exactly where he was by his breathing. "Samuel, your mother is very blessed to have such a fine, loyal son." He lay back down and sighed.

His words were not what I expected, so I didn't know how to answer. I listened to him sigh again, and swallow, and move his feet around. I didn't feel like asking him any more questions even though I could tell he wasn't asleep. Perhaps he was thinking about me being Mom's right-hand man. Maybe he was wondering how she was doing tonight with seven little kids in her house. Maybe he was missing his best friend.

I didn't want to think any more, so I lay down too. Eventually, sleep would come. But in the meantime, I stared at the tent flaps. First I prayed that Jill's dad would go away, then I prayed that he wouldn't.

We arrived home long after the sun had set. The house was completely dark except for a dim light in the living room. That's how our house looks when everyone is tucked in bed.

"They must all be asleep," Jill's dad said. "Do you have your key?"

"Yes."

"In the morning have your mom call me. I'll take her out for breakfast."

"Okay."

My insides were doing ups and downs, ups for the terrific words he had said about me during the campfire last night, and downs because I knew he had kissed Mom. Now he was staring at my house like he wished the lights would come on and Mom would appear at the front door.

"I've been thinking," he said. "I want you to hear me out before you go in the house."

"Okay."

"You are the oldest son in a fatherless home."

"I know that."

"You are Joanna's right-hand man, confidant, protector, and so on."

"Yes, I am."

He took a deep breath. "I really like Joanna a lot. She's become, uh, special to me."

I felt my fingers begin to wiggle against the van door.

"I plan to keep seeing her."

My fingers twitched harder.

"If some day I should want to marry her, this is how I would proceed."

I held my breath.

"I would come to you, and I would ask you for your stamp of approval on our marriage."

What a rotten thing to do to a kid.

"You would need to give me this approval, or blessing—whatever you want to call it—before I would marry Joanna. You would act as a brother or father in this matter, since she has neither, and you are the oldest son."

I found the door handle with my hand.

"When you give me your approval, you will abdicate your position to me."

"What position?"

"Male head of the house."

"*Abdi*-what?"

"Abdicate. When I marry her, you will become my son, and I will treat you as such."

"What does that mean?"

"It means you will answer to me as a son, and I will raise you as if I were your father."

"I will have to obey you?"

"Yes."

I never had to obey a man before—at least, not since my dad. "What's in it for me?"

He reached over and put his hand on my shoulder. "That's what you have to think about. A husband for your mom, and a father for you and your sister and brothers. I will do my best." He took a breath. "When you abdicate to someone, it is *your* choice. You choose to abdicate, and then you accept the results. It's a decision that requires much thought and maturity."

I shook his hand off my shoulder and got out of the van. He didn't drive off until I opened the front door of the house, threw my gear inside, and shut the door behind me.

First, I washed up. Then I went into Mom's room and told her I was home, and that she should call Jill's dad in the morning so he could take her out for breakfast. She opened one eye and smiled. Then I went to my room.

I found my dictionary buried under Karin's old rock collection in my closet. I carried the book to my bed so I could find the word: *Abdicate: to give up power or rights.*

I stayed in bed 'til late the next morning and tried to forget about abdicating to Jill's dad. He wanted me to say, "You're the boss"? No way.

A white-haired lady I'd never seen before stuck her head in my doorway and said, "It's ten-thirty. Pretty soon dandelions will sprout between your toes if you don't get up." She disappeared.

What? I sat up and listened. I heard cartoons going on the TV, and voices in the kitchen: Karin's and George Washington's, and—Emmie's? And the white-haired lady's? Who was she? Where was Mom? Why was Emmie still here?

Robin stood in the doorway. "Gramma has beckfrast ready," she said.

"I'll be there in a minute."

She went back to the kitchen.

I lay down again. I didn't want to think about *beckfrast* or strange *grammas* or . . .

I heard a familiar car, or van, pull up at our house. I peeked out through the edge of my curtain. Jill's dad walked around the side of the van and opened the door so Mom could get out. I was struck by how fresh and pretty she looked as she stepped out of the van, and then I noticed something that made me clench my fists. Jill's dad was struck too. I could tell by the way he paused before he took Mom's hand. He was in love. His movements gave it away, and so did the smile on his face as he looked down at her. I tried to push it out of my mind, to say it couldn't be so, but there it was, right in front of my eyes—love. I hated it. I hated him. I went back to my bed.

Chapter Six
Lassie

I needed to take the bull by the horns. I needed to get everything straightened out the way it used to be, with Mom raising us alone and me being her right-hand man. I needed to clear away the intruder, Jill's dad, and all his kids. They were muddling up my life.

But for now, I was part of a "coordinated effort." Mom was taking Karin, Jill, George Washington, and Blake to buy new shoes, since they all had holes in their toes. That left me, Emmie, and Natalie. We sat in the car with Jill's dad while he waited for Robin's class to end. Then he was going to drive me to Mike's birthday party and take the other kids to his house 'til Mom got back.

"Can we go on the bike rack?" Natalie asked her dad. "We need to practice gymnastics."

He nodded, so the girls got out and ran to the bike rack.

I decided to sit in the car and watch some kids who were bouncing a ball out on the playground. Jill's dad told me that this place was a school for the hearing impaired. Since Robin could hear fairly well with her new hearing aids, she came here just once a week to help make up for some of the phonics work she had missed before.

Now, while I was alone with Jill's dad, I needed to tell him to go away. I cleared my throat.

So did he. "Sam," he said.

I gulped. What if he was going to take the bull by the horns first?

"Do you remember the talk we had the night I brought you home from the father-son overnighter?"

How could I forget that?

"Do you?"

"Yes, sir."

"What are your thoughts, then?"

"About what?"

"I would like to marry Joanna."

Boy, I call that taking the bull by the horns! I dove out of the car lickity-split, and I ran to the bike racks where Emmie and Natalie played. But my desire to play was gone. I sat, alone, and watched two little girls climb on the bars while my mind twirled in anger and hopelessness. If I said no to Jill's dad, what would he do? Would he overrule me? Would he grab Mom and elope? Would he ditch us all?

I decided to stick to my guns. I had asked God to find a good husband for Mom. Maybe God needed Jill's dad to go away so the real guy could come along and take his place.

I looked at Jill's dad as he sat in the car. His eyes were shut. Was he praying? He opened his eyes and rubbed his forehead. I looked away. Maybe I would feel better after I got to Mike's house. Maybe not.

I avoided Jill's dad after that. Whenever I heard his van pull up in the drive, I went downstairs to listen to music and work on my airplane models. He came over almost every day, as he'd done for a long time now, so I got a lot of work done on my models.

Then we went on our picnic. We drove into the woods and parked beside a little dusty cabin. Jill's dad went inside first so he could swat the critters out with a broom. Then he opened the doors and windows and invited us all in.

The cabin was one big room with steps going up to a loft. The downstairs was large, with a kitchen at one end and a fireplace and couch at the other. There was no TV.

"Come on," Jill said to Karin. "The games are upstairs."

I followed the kids up because I had a feeling Mom and Jill's dad would stay downstairs. I was right. They sat on the couch and talked while the rest of us spread out all over the loft.

Karin, Jill, and I couldn't agree on which game to play: Monopoly, Tiddlywinks, or Uncle Wiggly. Finally, we combined the three into Uncle-Monopoly-Winks, which consisted of winning money every time your tiddlywink knocked a house off the Uncle Wiggly board.

Then we walked to the lake. Mom had brought our beach stuff and a good lunch, so we spent the afternoon there. While the little kids were splashing in the shallow water, I decided to go check out the sailboats along the dock. Jill's dad followed me.

We sat on the dock and hung our feet over the edge. The dock was brand new and freshly painted. There was still a pile of wood scraps sitting nearby. "Someone has been working hard on this dock," I said. I needed to talk about docks.

"It looks that way."

These were the first words we'd spoken to each other in over two weeks. I swung my legs so he would think I wasn't nervous.

"What are we going to do, Sam?"

We?

He cleared his throat.

"I don't want to talk about it now," I said.

Someone whined.

I looked around. There was no one near us. I heard the whine again. "What was that whining noise?" I asked.

Jill's dad looked around too.

We followed the noise to the bushes near the path. As we explored the path, we came upon a dog, a collie, lying on her side. When she saw us, she growled in a low rumble.

"I wonder why she doesn't get up," I said.

As if to prove me wrong, she struggled to her feet, putting all her weight on three legs and leaving her left hind leg to dangle. She whined softly and lay back down.

Jill's dad knelt beside her. When he reached toward her, she growled; so he pulled back. Her hair was tangled like Karin's is when she first wakes up. "I wish I had my gloves," Jill's dad mumbled.

The dog growled at him.

I reached toward the dog 'til my hand was near her nose. She didn't growl at me, probably because I'm a kid.

"Move your hand slowly until she smells it, and then try to scratch her behind the ears," Jill's dad said.

I did as told, and she let me rub her gently in the soft, unmatted fur there. "She has a collar on." I felt its edges deeply hidden in her mane. I tried to feel around for some tags but found only a buckle.

She stretched out stiffly on her side.

"Is she old?" I asked.

He reached toward her nose now. "Talk to her softly. Keep rubbing her ears." She allowed him to check her teeth and the skin under her eyes. His hands moved slowly along her body.

"Easy, Lassie," I said softly. "Your ears are so silky. Easy, girl. Is she a girl?"

"Yes. You're doing a good job. Keep her calm. She's not really old, just hurting."

I continued to stroke her and talk.

His hand moved to her sore foot, and when he touched it, she flinched and growled. He continued to rub his hand along her hind leg, slowly, gently, while I kept her calm. She flinched again and bared her teeth.

Jill's dad sat back on his heels. "The leg is broken," he said. "I wonder if a car hit her."

"What'll we do?" I asked. "Who do we call? She has no tags on her collar."

"I'll bet she lives around here. She looks well cared for." He scratched his chin. "Let's set the bone."

"Put it in a cast? Here?"

"No." He looked around. "Maybe a splint . . . "

"There's wood slats in that pile by the dock."

". . . and something to tie . . ."

"Paint rags—I saw paint rags."

He stood up. "You stay here with, uh, Lassie."

"Okay."

He came back with several wood slats and a pile of rags.

He twisted a rag into a long strip. "You keep rubbing Lassie's ears while I fix her a muzzle." He fashioned the strip into a loop and slipped it gently over her long nose. "The blessings of a collie," he said quietly. "Thank you, Lord."

I never heard anybody thank the Lord before on account of a dog's long, skinny nose. Jill's dad was busy arranging wood slats and more rag strips. Slowly, carefully, he slid one of the slats, with a rag beneath it, under the dog's leg. She flinched and growled. He stopped for a few minutes.

Then he leaned toward her again. "She's not going to like this," he said to me. "She may twist sideways to resist us. If she does, you keep her muzzle on and hold her down until I say otherwise."

I leaned my weight over her.

"Press your knee on top of her shoulder lightly. She'll feel secure with you there, and you'll have a way to hold her down, if necessary."

I did as he said and continued to rub her beautiful head.

"She's a fine animal." Jill's dad was holding her leg with both hands now, manipulating his thumbs along the leg.

I stopped watching at that point because Lassie tried to get up. She growled and jerked hard, so I flattened my knee against her to hold her down. As I moved forward I grabbed the muzzle just as she reached it with her paw to push it off her nose.

Jill's dad stopped her paw long enough for me to get the muzzle secure on her face. His knee was on her too.

"Easy, girl," I said to the dog. "Easy, girl." I began to stroke her shoulder and her back and her ears. She settled down.

Jill's dad went back to his work. I couldn't watch because of my position, so I just rested on top of Lassie, or whoever she was, and talked to her 'til Jill's dad said he was done.

When we got off her, she immediately sprang up, shook the muzzle free, and took off through the woods. Even though she did not rest her weight on the splinted leg, she was out of our sight in a few seconds.

"You're welcome," Jill's dad said to the bushes.

"She definitely had somewhere to go," I said.

"There's a row of cabins over the hill." Jill's dad brushed off his clothes and turned to me. "Let's get back to Joanna and the kids."

"Fine." I was glad he didn't want to stay and talk about me abdicating and him marrying Mom-Jo. I took a peek at him as he walked alongside me. He had just performed free veterinary services on a dog who couldn't say "Thank you." He had given me respect when I said I didn't want to talk about the problem.

I looked ahead again. Why couldn't he be rich so I could like him?

Chapter Seven
Scratch the Pudding

Chocolate pudding is everyone's favorite at our house, and I knew that sooner or later we would have it when Jill's family came to supper. They usually came twice a week. Mom just cooked double of whatever it was she had planned to make anyway. We made the table big, added the card table going into the hall, and we were in business. Most of the time Jill's family got there early enough to help get everything set up, and the day we had chocolate pudding was no exception.

I had asked to help that day, because I love Mom's pudding and I needed to make sure I gave myself one of the good dishes. You might call this selfish, but I call it honest. The only problem was, I wasn't the only one who thought of it.

Since it was the Friday before Jill's dad's birthday, Mom decided to use our pretty dishes. Along with them came the fancy glass dishes that looked so terrific with Mom's satiny, cool, smooth chocolate pudding piled inside. She called it "scratch pudding" because she made it from scratch. I always liked to watch her do it. Then she'd let me pour it into the pretty dishes, all ten of them, and then put 'em in the refrigerator to cool. Jill's dad had never tasted Mom's scratch pudding before. He was in for a big treat.

As usual, Jill's dad helped set up the tables. Together we put out the silverware and dishes and salt and pepper and all that kind of stuff. When that was ready, we put out the pudding. I tried not to look too obvious when I examined the dishes to see which one had the most in it. And I tried not to notice when he did the same thing.

While we were doing all of this, Natalie went over and sat in the corner with Bongo and a box of dog biscuits. She clutched a dog biscuit in her little fist and held it in front of his face. Bongo went crazy trying to lick through her fingers to reach the biscuit. She giggled.

Bongo whined.

Her dad stopped what he was doing. "Natalie," he said, "stop teasing the dog."

"He likes it," she said. "Look at how he slobbers all over my fingers."

"Give him the biscuit."

She opened her hand.

Bongo grabbed the biscuit and ran off with it. Natalie followed him.

After we'd gone back into the kitchen, I thought I heard a noise in the dining room. I peeked in to see Jill and Karin rearranging the puddings so they had the best ones. They left.

I went back and made sure mine was still the biggest. I couldn't tell if mine was the same or not, but George Washington's looked bigger than mine, so I switched with him and left. Little kids don't need as much anyway.

From the kitchen I could hear little noises coming from the dining room again. I peeked in. There was Natalie, examining every single pudding at the table. I don't know if she moved any or not, because she had finished doing whatever it was she'd done. Then she wandered out to the hall.

Blake entered and did a silent walk around the table, stopping to stare into each individual bowl of pudding. Mom needed me to go get the milk, so I didn't see Blake finish his survey. When I peeked back into the dining room, he was gone.

So I checked my pudding for the last time, switched a few dishes around, decided I had the one I wanted, and went outside to gather the kids in.

They were busy playing our latest invention, tensketball, which was actually basketball played with tennis balls, since our basketball had gone flat. Actually, tensketball was a lot of fun because Jill's dad had given us a whole bag of tennis balls, and we used them all at once. If two kids on the same team threw their tennis balls up into the hoop at the same time, they got four points; and if both kids got under the hoop in time for the balls to bounce down on their heads, the points were doubled. It took me a while to get everybody in for supper because they kept wanting to throw one more time, and when we did get inside, we were all sweaty—all except for Mom and Jill's dad. I noticed they were both cleaned up like they were going someplace. Only I knew they weren't because nobody had asked me to babysit.

Since I'm Mom's right-hand man, I gave thanks. Everyone said, "Amen."

We ate chicken and potatoes and green beans. It all tasted good, but the best part was looking at my rich brown pudding in its shiny little glass dish. We were trying to learn good table manners, so Mom made us all wait 'til everyone was finished before we cleared the dirty plates and put the pudding dishes front and center.

"This is scratch pudding," Karin said proudly.

"That must mean it's made from scratch, right?" Jill's dad asked Mom.

"Right."

Robin and Natalie were pushing each other, both trying to get the same fork. "It's mine," Natalie said.

"Mine," Robin answered.

Robin pulled her hearing aids out, laid them beside her plate, and looked Natalie directly in the face. "Mine." She shut her eyes.

I handed Natalie the fork that was sitting under her arm.

"Oh," she said quietly. Nobody really needed a fork anyway to eat pudding. Sometimes girls don't make any sense. Robin opened her eyes.

Natalie looked at Mom. "Do you scratch when you make this pudding?" she asked politely.

I smiled. Natalie always asked interesting questions at the table.

"No, dear."

Karin said loudly, "I used to think it was called scratch pudding because you itch when you make it."

"Well," Natalie asked. "Does it make you scratch after you eat it, then? When does it make you scratch?"

Karin and Jill laughed out loud.

I took a bite of my wonderful pudding and let it slide around in my mouth.

Jill's dad straightened Natalie out. "This pudding is called scratch pudding because it didn't come out of a box. It was made with ingredients like flour and eggs and milk, all stirred together."

"Oh," Natalie said, a bit angrily, probably because Karin and Jill were both laughing and scratching.

Robin accidentally bumped Natalie's arm.

"Stop it, dummy!" Natalie yelled, even though Robin couldn't hear her. Then Natalie looked into her pudding dish. "Hey," she said bluntly. "This isn't my pudding."

I took my second bite. It was like having a party in my mouth. "Great pudding, Mom," I said.

"Thank you, dear."

Jill's dad set down his spoon. "How do you know that isn't your pudding?" he asked Natalie.

Jill also set her spoon down. "Oh-oh," she said quietly.

I took my third bite.

"Natalie," said her dad in the sternest voice I had ever heard him use. "Did you stir your pudding?"

Natalie didn't answer him, but she frowned.

"Natalie, did you take the biggest pudding and stir it?"

She looked at the table.

"Oh, yuck!" Jill cried. "She did it again! She stirred her pudding with her finger so nobody else would want it!"

"But this isn't mine," Natalie said.

I remembered switching the puddings around *after* Natalie had visited the table. Had I shifted her pudding somewhere? Had I shifted it to myself? I set my spoon down.

"Natalie, when did you stir your pudding?" her dad asked her.

"Before we all sat down to eat," she said quietly. She was beginning to look kind of scared.

"Did you wash your hands after you played with the dog?"

"Sort of."

"What is sort of?" His words came through tight lips.

"The, uh, bathroom door was locked shut, so I wiped my hands on my shirt instead of using water and stuff."

Blake threw down his spoon. "Oh, sick!" he said. "I switched the puddings all around after I saw her leave the dining room."

Spoons dropped like little metal bombs all over the place.

"Who did you give Natalie's pudding to, Blake?" Mom asked.

"I don't remember."

I spoke up. "I switched them again after Blake."

Jill's dad addressed Natalie. "Young lady, you go into the room with the piano, and shut the door. I'll come deal with you in a few minutes."

One by one the kids left the table. I just sat there and felt sick while I watched Robin, who was the only person to finish her pudding. Her hearing aids were beside her plate where they did no good. She was enjoying a nice dessert. I looked the other way. Mom, Jill's dad, and I listened to Robin set her spoon down. I saw the movement of her hand as she picked up her little glass dish. She was probably going to lick the inside like I usually did.

"May I be excused?" I said.

"Yes," Mom answered.

Robin got up from the table and picked up her hearing aids. She went to her dad so he could help her get them back in. I carried a pile of dishes out to the kitchen. While I was there I heard Mom say to Jill's dad, "Well, Romeo, these romantic dinners are too much."

I heard Jill's dad laugh, and then he got up to go deal with a little, scared pudding stirrer who waited in the other room.

Later that night, I rolled over in my bed and listened. Jill's dad was still here. I heard his voice in the living room. I wished I could hear the words. Soon, he carried his sleeping girls out, shut the front door, and drove off. I was glad he was gone. Now I could go to sleep.

I listened to Mom close up the back of the house and put something away in the refrigerator. I heard water running upstairs, followed by light switches being flicked in the hallway and Mom's room. I heard her go out on her balcony. Shouldn't she be in bed by now? I thought about the Romeo and Juliet comic book we had. Juliet stood out on the balcony and said, "Romeo, Romeo, wherefore art thou Romeo?"

I sat up. Was there something romantic going on out in our yard? Was Jill's dad out in the yard looking up at Mom's balcony? No. Old people don't do romantic stuff like that. I lay back down again. He'd kissed her before, and that was romantic. Maybe I'd better check this out.

I tiptoed upstairs in the darkness. No use in turning lights on and alarming Mom at this hour. I would simply peek at her, decide she was okay, and sneak back down to my room.

She was not hollering, "Romeo, Romeo," to anyone in the yard. She was sitting on the bench, crying her eyes out.

I decided to leave her alone.

When I got back into bed I tried to think of a reason for her crying. Did it have to do with her sisters being dead? Did it have to do with one of us kids? Did it have to do with Jill's dad? I decided that since he had just been here, it must have to do with him. Had he said something cruel to her? No. He didn't seem to have any cruelness inside of him to use on people. I lay back against my pillow for the millionth time.

"Lord," I said. "Things are kind of messed up around here. We need your help."

Chapter Eight
Back to Square One

We were back to square one. It was Mom-Jo and me, and just three other kids, like in the old days; but I'm not sure I liked it as much as I'd planned to. I missed going to Jill's house to catch toads and go fishing and do all that fun, messy stuff. I missed the babysitting money I used to earn when Mom went out with Jill's dad, and I missed her being happy. I wondered why he went away. I even asked Mom once why he didn't come around any more, and she said, "It was a mutual decision." I wasn't sure what that meant, and she didn't seem to want to talk about it, so I let it be. Two weeks passed. At least I didn't have to worry about abdicating anymore.

Even though I didn't ask Mom questions about Jill's dad, he seemed to be on my mind a lot. Sometimes Mom and I would be in the same room together, and I could tell we didn't want to look at each other in the eyes. I wanted to be her right-hand man, but I had this big black blob sitting inside of me whenever I was with her. I think I was worried that Jill's dad had left because of me.

I'd been having another sleepless night. Then I began dreaming that Jill's dad came to marry Mom and he couldn't find her. She was sitting on top of my basketball hoop, and he wouldn't look up. He just walked around in the driveway, but he wouldn't look up. I kept yelling, "Look up, stupid! She's on the basketball hoop! She's on the basketball hoop!" But the words made no noise when they came out of my mouth, and Jill's dad wandered around with his ladder under his arm. . . .

Bells were ringing.

I sat up in bed. No, it wasn't bells. It was the phone. Mom had picked it up in her bedroom. I remembered hearing the phone ring other nights recently, always real late. I decided to go upstairs and check it out. I tiptoed up the steps in the dark. Mom's door was shut, but there was a thin slice of light shining through the crack along the side. I pressed my ear against the door.

She was talking in a quiet voice, and then she stopped. In a few minutes she talked again. I wondered who would call her at this late hour, and then I didn't wonder. As I listened, I thought I heard her say Blake's name and Emmie's name. I pressed my ear closer. Mom was silent again. Then she said, "I think so too, Dan."

She didn't say much more, and after she hung up I sneaked back down to my bed. Why did he call her late at night? Why did he stop coming here and inviting us to his house? Why did he avoid us completely and then call Mom late at night? What was he doing?

Tomorrow, I would find out. I would get on my bike and go see Jill's dad. I would take the bull by the horns.

While I rode the three miles to Jill's house, I decided that my own house had been boring lately. I realized that I missed Jill because of the fierce competitor she was in all the sports we invented. For a girl, Jill had exceptional strength and speed. I missed Natalie because of the nosy questions she asked grown-ups all the time, and I missed Emmie because she liked to rub my back when I sat in the grass. I missed watching Robin be gentle with animals. I had to admit that I even missed Jill's dad. The silly things he did and his helpful attitude made Mom smile. I guess they made me smile too. And when he was with us, I felt . . . safe.

I got off my bike when I reached Jill's mailbox. There was a new sign there that read, ''Daniel R. Sanders, D.V.M.'' I went around back to the barn.

The barn was fixed up sparkly-nice. The trash was cleared out, the stalls were walled in, and the building had real floors and a ceiling. I could tell where the waiting room was because of the chairs in boxes. Beyond it was the first examination room, complete with table and instruments. I went on down the hall past a big storage area to a room that had rows of cages in varying sizes. So far, there were no customers.

''Can I help you?'' Jill's dad said behind me.

I wheeled around. He was wiping his hands on a paint rag. Both his ears had pencils parked over them, and his hair and glasses were speckled with white dots.

''You're polka dotted,'' I said.

I decided I liked him with white dots all over his face. In fact, all of a sudden I was filling up with good feelings that surprised me.

"Would you like a job?" he asked me.

I hadn't come for a job, but I might as well hear him out. "What kind of a job?"

"I'm going to hire an assistant. He'll need to help me take care of the animals that stay the night, hold animals when I work on them . . ." He looked down at his hands. ". . . paint walls."

"For money?"

"Yes. It's a real job, part-time. I'll need you on summer mornings, and as your schedule permits during the school year."

"Has anyone else applied?"

"The word's not out yet. I planned to come to you first."

"Why me?"

"I've seen your work."

"Oh, Lassie." I remembered the beautiful dog we had helped together. The picture in my mind calmed me.

He took off his glasses and tried to wipe them with the rag that was hanging out of his pocket. The speckles turned into snowy smears. "I'd better get some thinner on these." He turned to a tin container that was behind him on a shelf. He used the thinner to further mess up his glasses. When he put them back on his face, I thought they still looked a bit cloudy, but he kept them on anyway. I was struck by a new thought. He needed someone to take care of him. He needed someone like Mom to help him get the white glop off his glasses, and to help him paint, and to bring him lunch and talk to him. I was beginning to feel real bad that he wasn't hanging around our house anymore. Now I'd been side-tracked because he asked me to work for him and because I was watching him mess with his glasses. It was time to take the bull by the horns.

"Mr. Sanders," I said.

"Yes."

"I've been wondering why you don't come see us any-more."

"I've been setting up the clinic."

Well, he *had* done an awful lot of work. Now I was getting sidetracked again. Back to business. "Any other reason?"

He sighed and sat down on the table next to the thinner. "I'm contemplating what to do about a kid I know."

"Name the kid."

"Samuel Joseph Rogers."

I was getting scared. Maybe we'd better go back to the subject of the job. "Do I need to fill out an application?"

"You're hired. No application necessary."

Filling out an application would have given me some thinking time. "Is there any kind of a deal attached to this job?" I asked.

"What kind of a deal?"

"You give me a job, and I let you marry Mom. A deal like that." All of a sudden I realized that my feelings had changed about Jill's dad. Maybe I *wanted* him to marry Mom. Maybe I needed her to be happy again. If he was going to strike a deal like that, let him. I'd listen.

Even though my question was nervy, he accepted it flat out. I could tell he was thinking about it seriously. "There are no deals attached to the job," he said. "You work for me, and I pay you."

I was neither disappointed nor surprised. I was concerned. Maybe he wasn't interested in Mom anymore. Maybe he'd found himself another lady, one without kids. I began to feel real bad, sort of like when your ice cream falls off the cone and lands on your shoe, only this was much worse.

He spoke again. "Are you wondering why I've been contemplating what to do about the kid named Sam?"

"Sort of."

He took off his glasses again and laid them on the counter while he rubbed his eyes. "I love Sam's mother, and she loves me."

Thank goodness, I thought.

"This Sam kid doesn't want me to marry her."

"He never said that. He said he didn't want to abdicate."

He sighed. "I know what you mean."

How would he know what I meant? "I have a question about abdication."

"Let's hear it."

"What if, after I've abdicated, we disagree on something?"

"Such as—?"

"You say I go to bed at ten o'clock, and I think I should go to bed at eleven?"

He grinned. "I suppose we would have to discuss the matter and come up with a compromise."

"Like ten-thirty?"

"Possibly, and use it as a testing ground. If ten-thirty bedtimes turn you into a morning grouch-bear, then you would need to go back to the earlier time. As your father-person, I would need to enforce it." He looked thoughtful for a moment. "And sometimes a dad has to say a flat no because he is responsible to God for his kids' upbringing. If a guy loves his kids, he'll have to say no to some things, sort of like putting your knee on a dog so you can fix his leg. Then when you let him go, he's prepared for life."

I looked down at the floor. There were paint spatters on his shoes and socks.

"I want you to look at me right in the eye and tell me why you don't want me to marry your mom."

I couldn't.

"What are you afraid of losing?"

"I can't put it into words."

"Are things right between you and Joanna?" he asked.

"We're fine." No, we weren't.

"Are you uncomfortable around her because you know something isn't right?"

I didn't answer.

"Sam?"

"What?"

"Go home and talk to your mom."

My legs were getting awful tired from riding to Jill's house and back. But the distance gave me good thinking time. Jill's dad was right. I should go talk to Mom. In fact, I should've talked to her a long time ago. I'd been dwelling on me and my worries about Jill's dad. I really hadn't paid much attention to what was going on in Mom's head.

When I got home, Mom was upstairs drawing umbrellas. The kids were outside, I guess, and the air still smelled of tomato soup for lunch. Jill's dad had given me a peanut butter and banana sandwich. It wasn't my favorite meal, but I must admit it stuck real good in my stomach. I felt like I wouldn't be hungry again for months.

"When you're gone so long, you need to phone me so I know where you are," Mom said when I entered the room.

"I forgot," I answered. "I won't do it again. Sorry." I sat down on the extra stool beside the light table. "I went to see Mr. Sanders."

"I know. He called me."

"He did?"

"Yes. He said you'd been to see him and that you were on your way home."

"What else did he say?"

"That's all. He was afraid I may have been worrying about where you were, so he called."

"Oh. I need to talk to you."

She set her pen down and faced me. "I need to talk to you too."

I took a deep breath. How would I begin? "Mr. Sanders hasn't been coming to see us for two reasons."

"Okay. Name them."

"One, he's working on his new clinic. It's going to be real nice, but he's a lousy painter. He's got paint dots all over his glasses and clothes."

Mom smiled. "The other reason?"

"He's been waiting for me because I didn't want him to marry you. I didn't want to have a dad to boss me around."

"You're using the word *didn't*."

"I think I'm changing my mind."

"What is making you change your mind?"

"I guess I miss having him around and doing all the fun stuff we do when our families are together."

"You mean like stirring the pudding?" Mom laughed.

"Yeah," I said with a smile. "And I think I'd like you to have him too. You miss him. Don't you?"

"Yes."

"Do you love him?"

"Yes."

"And he loves you?"

"Yes."

"So why did you guys split up just because of a kid?"

"He didn't tell you?"

"No."

Mom faced me. "He didn't want to barge right in and take over your life." She put her arms on my shoulders. "You are so very important to me, and that makes you important to Dan too. He holds you in high regard, not only because you're my son, but because, in many ways, you remind him of himself when he was your age."

"He never said anything to me about it."

"He wanted you to come to your own decision without him influencing you. And he said you needed time to get adjusted to the new ideas you were being hit with."

They must have talked about me a lot. I felt my face get hot.

Mom gave my shoulder a little rub. I knew she liked me an awful lot. "When Dan was your age, he didn't have a father either. His father died when he was nine. His mother began to see another man, and Dan got angry about it. He was the only son, and he didn't want a stranger coming into his life, into his father's spot. Dan said he acted terrible around the guy: used foul language, caused all sorts of problems.''

"Jill's dad did that?" It was hard enough imagining him as a kid, let alone a bratty one.

"He drove his mother's friend away."

"So then he was glad, I suppose."

"For a while. But as he got older he realized that his mom was going to be lonely for the rest of her life. The kids are grown now, and his mom is alone."

"I never thought of that."

"Now he feels guilty because he acted so selfishly. That was before he became a Christian, and since then the Lord has helped him change. So, he left us—sort of—for a while. He said it would give you time to think. He said, 'You can't just march out and grab what you want. Sometimes you have to be patient.' ''

"But he still called you late at night."

"That's right. He loves me."

I shut my mouth so my mind could do some thinking. Mom picked up her pen and began to darken the lines on her umbrella. Jill's dad didn't want me to make the same mistake he had made? He and Mom were waiting for me?

"Mom?"

"Yes, dear."

"Maybe one of us should go talk to Mr. Sanders."

"What should we tell him?"

"Tell him it's okay for you guys to get married." Something that could have been excitement fluttered inside of me.

She put the pen back in its holder.

"How about if I stay here with the kids while you go tell him," I said.

She smiled, gave me a great big hug, and walked out the door.

This was going to be a good day, even though we were never going to be rich.

I don't know how many people get married with eight kids standing all around them, but Mom and Jill's dad did. And when I think of who all those kids were, I was surprised at how smoothly everything went.

Jill and Karin got all dressed up real fancy like *they* were the bride, and George Washington and Blake made it through the ceremony without fighting, which wasn't how it looked, because Blake's face had a big red mark on it from sleeping on his Tonka earthmover. Emmie leaned against me the whole time, which was okay, because now she was going to be my little sister. Natalie managed to get through the whole deal with only one interrupting question: "Will I still get as much stuff for Christmas?"—which we all ignored. Robin kept her ears in and stood intently through the whole thing.

After the ceremony was over, we ate cake, and we watched Mom and Jill's dad open some gifts, all boring stuff like dishes and blankets.

I thought things were going to get exciting when George Washington dropped his ring into the punch bowl. Blake, who was always ready to help out, started to roll up his sleeve. He was going to rescue the ring. I sent Karin to go get Mom, who was talking to Lulu's sister in the doorway. As Karin got to her, I saw Jill's dad reach the punch bowl.

He leaned down and whispered to my brothers. Then he winked at Mom, who was looking worried. I saw her relax as Blake rolled his sleeve back into place. Jill's dad walked by me on his way to the doorway. "After this is all over," he said to me, "help Grandma find the ring."

"Okay."

When the relatives and Lulu had gone, Jill's grandma carried her suitcases out to the van, because she was going to take us all to Jill's house for a few days while the new couple went on their honeymoon.

Jill's dad cornered me in the church coatroom. "Just some last minute instructions," he said.

"Okay."

"The people who own the two dogs we're boarding know the situation and that you're in charge."

"Okay."

"Check the dogs several times a day, and keep the kids away from them—except Robin. She has a calming effect. She can be your assistant."

"Okay."

"I wrote a list and hung it beside Fifi's cage." He smiled at me. We both thought Fifi was a stupid name for a basset hound.

"I'll check the list."

"Grandma Sanders has the phone number if a problem comes up. She can reach me."

"Okay."

He reached out and took my hand. We shook.

For some reason, I couldn't make my mouth work, so I just shook his hand and let go. He reached into his pocket and pulled something out, clutched in his fist. "I have a gift for you, something I won once. It has sentimental value. I would like to pass it on to you, my oldest son.''

He reached out his hand and dropped the steely marble into my palm. Then he went out the door.

Sometimes you have to take the bull by the horns. And sometimes, I guess, when other people are involved, you have to pray, then wait a bit and stare the bull in the face for a while before the encounter is finished. Or begun.